A

HISTORY

OF

VIOLENCE

MALLORY FOX

A History of Violence
(A Violent Agenda Book One)

Copyright © May 2021 by Mallory Fox

Published in the United Kingdom by
Black Jade Publishing Ltd.

Editing by Indie Hub
Proofing by Lea Joan
Cover Design by Vicious Desires Design

To Steph & Nicola.
Thank you for making this special edition beautiful, dark, and deadly...
just like V

MALLORY FOX

A History of Violence

Fire burns the worst sins. Trust is overrated.
Killing for pleasure is messy, bloody, chaotic....

He was supposed to die.

But now I have him where I want him, I can't help but taste him a little.

All of them.

They've gotten under my skin. These Sacred Heart boys.

The way they look at me, a need, a hunger clawing inside, I recognize it in the mirror. It's their eyes. They tell me they don't give a fuck if they live or die. That I'm the prey and they're the carnivores. That they're soulless.

But in the end, they all beg.
Violent, bloody, and raw.
Because I'm the real monster.

They just don't know it yet.

AUTHOR'S NOTE

A History of Violence is a serial killer bully romance intended for mature audiences. Some scenes contain graphic violence and potentially triggering moments. Please read at your own discretion.

Love & All Things Dark,
Mallory
❤

PROLOGUE

HOW DOES *it feel to kill?*

Excitement. Adrenaline. There's a split second, a moment you're on the edge, staring right into the eyes of your obsession when the emotions burn. A dark thrill spills through your veins. Sounds are louder. Seconds are longer.

You close your eyes, drag air into your lungs, and sigh as you move closer.

She smells so fucking good.

She knows it's coming. You told them it would fucking happen, but they didn't listen. You never meant to hurt anyone? Bullshit right there. Stupidly, she believed you, that you never wanted any of this. That you never asked for it. You didn't want to cross that line... But you never had a choice.

They didn't listen.

Now look.

She's absolutely fucking terrified. Her fear ignites a fire within as she begs. Her words do nothing to stop you as you twist the hilt of the knife in, and the unrelenting metal buries deep inside her softness. So soft. So weak. Her pathetic cries do nothing to halt the warm blood as it spills over your clenched fingers.

It just...intensifies everything.

7

Your eyes travel to the place where the blade is nestled lovingly. The metallic tang of blood sears your nose and fills your lungs. She tries to speak one last time. You kiss her bloody lips, suffocating whatever she was going to say, and stare into her eyes only to see love reflected back. It was always there, wasn't it?

Love is the reason you need to do this.

So, how does it feel to kill someone you love?

It feels fucking liberating.

ONE

VIOLA

THE WORST SOUND in the world is when a guy begs. I hate it. I really do. Men are pathetic, but even more so when they're shit-scared, strung by their limbs, and bound completely naked to my killing table.

This guy isn't begging.

He's not even talking.

He's watching me with hazy, unfocused eyes while the shed load of alcohol and drugs in his system continues to cloud his judgment. Until his eyes flutter closed again, and his breathing dips.

Fuck.

I slap him harder. He doesn't stir.

I might have dosed him a little too much. I've had to slap him awake multiple times. I hope he doesn't die of an opiate overdose before I make him suffer, because this one is a piece of shit.

Young, innocent girls. That's what he likes. He likes to knock young girls around before knocking them up. Young girls like me. Good job I've spruced this one really well, like a pig fit for roasting. The restraints are slicing into his arms and neck, holding the bastard still for me on the mattress of the bed I charmed him onto. Built like a freight train—all muscle and sinew and veins popping out everywhere, he could crush me with one hand and that's not even trying. I felt no qualms injecting him with my signature cocktail of drugs. I needed to be extra careful.

Now, he can't hurt a fly.

Because he's fucking crashing on me.

Great.

I sigh, letting all the tension spill out of my body in one forceful breath, and look around the room for something that might help me wake him up. This is Dante's cabin, after all. He lets me use it for the *black days* when he's away working. I do not know where he goes when he works. He doesn't tell me. I never ask. I should get my own place. This place has his energy all over it, seeped into the walls and furniture. *But where else would I fucking go?* Who else has a cabin off-grid with rolls of plastic sheeting in the basement and shit loads of drugs in the bathroom cabinet?

Bathroom.

I get up off the bed and walk into the en-suite and open the cabinet below the sink. Sure enough, there's a nasal spray bottle tucked in the back that looks like it might be what I need. I check the label and read the instructions to make sure it's the right one because that would be fucking annoying if it wasn't, before going back into the bedroom to straddle the fucker and spray a shot up his nose.

Nothing happens.

I run my eyes over the label again.

Was I supposed to inject it? I've no fucking clue.

I'm going to have to call Dante, of all people, and tell him his shitty drugs aren't working. If the guy stops breathing before I've even got what I need, that would be bad. A strained sigh leaves my lips again, fogging the frigid air in front of my mouth. It's fucking freezing in here, but that's to be expected. This house is off grid.

Fucking piece of shit. He can't even get through one night with me. *What kind of weak-ass pussy does that make him?*

I slap him again, harder.

He groans and the guy's eyes startle open. He looks right at me, confusion washing over his features as he blinks, taking me and his surroundings in. I must be a pretty sight because he slowly grins, his face creasing into a disgusting leer. He doesn't seem bothered about the ligatures top and tail. Obviously, this one isn't scared of one little girl in a farmhouse bedroom with patterned sheets and floral wallpaper.

He thinks I'm his next target.

How fucking quaint.

He's mine.

"Well, look at you. Aren't you a sight for sore eyes, baby? Come here."

He has no fucking clue. It sends a slight thrill down my spine.

Sometimes they panic. Sometimes they beg.

I love it most when they think they're in control because, of all things, they're never that.

He blinks again, grinning in the dim light of the main cabin bedroom, seeing my calming brown, almond-shaped eyes, a slash of red for lips, and a cascade of pale blonde hair, almost white, over an under-developed body. He sees my lacy white underwear. My mixed ethnicity makes me exotic. My youthful looks make me seem underage. I look like someone's shy niece who wouldn't say boo to a goose, all dressed in her smalls for her first fucking time, not the demon bitch that I really am.

I wanted him awake for this, but I can't let my guard down. The dark fury that fills my entire world when it comes—even if it feels so damn good—can't be let out today. Even if the relief is like a heaviness lifting, like coming out of the depths of a hell buried so deep, like clawing a way back to sanity, I need to keep my wits about me.

I need to make it last.

I let a shy smile play over my lips and run my hand over my

13

victim's taut chest as his eyes burn holes into my soul, trying not to let the flutters of excitement creep under my skin at what I'm about to do. His whole body relaxes, as though he understands why he's here. The void inside is ready. It's waited a long time for this.

Too long.

I tried to be good. I really did. But this fucker just had to land on my desk. They were going to charge him. Luckily, I got to him before the police could.

He moans as my hand glides down his abs, over his stomach, and stops at the thin trail of hair that leads to his cock. The Naloxone has helped. He's standing perfectly to attention now. Disgustingly rock hard. This kinky setup must be doing it for him. I wasn't sure. I pegged him as the type of guy who prefers it quick and furious in the back of his shitty Beemer, in an alleyway, or even the other way round—me tied up and him with the knife.

Fuck. Like that would ever happen.

My phone beeps, letting me know I have a message. It's Dante or my employer. No one else has this number. Dante would never disturb me on a bad day unless he was tipping me off. He knows I need absolute calm to fill the void. He knows because he has one just like it.

Glancing down, I read the notification quickly so as not to spoil my mood.

I was right.

The message is from my employer. Two words that mean more to me than I care to admit.

New job.

A fleeting emotion of relief stirs in the pit of my stomach. Ignoring it, I squash it down and take hold of the rapist's dick roughly with my free hand and squeeze hard. He groans. I can't tell if it's from lust or if my nails digging in have hurt him. Another emotion stirs. Disgust at this pig of a man. Disgust at what I'm doing.

Candles flicker. Shadows flit across the wooden walls, chasing the dark.

Pity. Hate. Loathing. It all creeps over me until the sickness inside threatens to swallow me down into a red mist and completely take control. I've worked too long and hard stalking this one to let it. I suck in the icy air and force myself to stare into his dark, almost pitch-black, eyes that look completely feral in this light. He's not a man. He's an animal. One that can't control his urges. An animal who can't even control his dick.

One that needs to be put out of his misery.

It doesn't take long before he's throbbing in my palm. My entire body tenses like it wants to reject the feeling of him, sick to my stomach at how easily I turn him on. There's a flash of hunger, a desire for more, in his eyes. Not fear or uncertainty. Pure, unadulterated desire. I try to match his look.

I'm good at being a mirror.

His lips curl into a snarl. "If you wanted it so badly, love, you only had to ask." He pulls on his restraints. "You didn't have to go to all this trouble though, baby doll. Untie me. I won't hurt you."

I say nothing, squeezing extra hard, pumping him a little more with my nails buried in his shaft. The movement makes his eyes roll back and drool forms in the corner of his mouth.

"Hey. Nice and easy, baby," he winces. "Careful with those nails of yours."

Fuck. I'm such a tease… aren't I? But I'm not here to fuck him. Just play. *Maybe cut his dick off and make him eat it.*

"It's cute, you think this is foreplay," I finally say, inclining my head.

He smirks, irritating me with arrogance. "Untie me. I'll show you foreplay."

I shake my head. "No."

"It's better when I'm on top. Untie me, let me show you how good I can make you feel."

"I prefer you like this. See it as roleplay."

"Roleplay? Does that turn you on, baby?"

I open the lower bedside drawer and take out the electrical tape I know Dante keeps there. I also take out a pair of scissors and cut a piece of the tape while he watches me.

"What game are you playing, little girl?"

I finish prepping the tape and take out the scalpel. Twisting the metal handle in my fingers so he can see. His eyes narrow.

"Is this like doctors and nurses shit?"

I press the icy blade to my lips and look down at my prey, letting him see the calmness in my eyes.

"I'll play doctors and nurses if I get to be the surgeon," I say.

I move my hand back to his shaft and tighten it, pulling it taut. Then I move my other hand, knife hilt tight in my palm until the pointed end rests on his lower abdomen. The dickhead strains under my touch as I continue to draw the blade down, but he hardly moves an inch. The five-point restraint is holding him quite nicely.

His eyes narrow. "Careful with that. Little girls shouldn't play with knives."

He still doesn't know. As I said, I don't look scary.

He doesn't see the darkness inside.

"Is that what you said to Milly?" I ask. *Milly Jones. Barely fifteen years old.*

"Milly? Who the fuck is Milly? Is she a friend of yours? Two of you here to play, huh?" He glances at the door.

"Milly Jones," I say, helpfully.

His brow furrows. This isn't how the game is supposed to go. "Am I supposed to know the bitch?"

"You should. You picked her up after school last week. St Margaret's." *Raped and mutilated her with a scalpel in a nearby park. Left her for dead. She's lucky to be alive.*

Lucky for me, she remembered his license plate. It led me to Dr. Paedo here.

"Oh, that cunt." Humor flashes over his features. "Fucking bitch," he chuckles, still oblivious to his predicament. "She was asking for it."

"Was she? Were they all…"—I let the knife blade play slowly over his skin— "asking for it?"

I nick his skin, drawing blood. His face twists into something ugly, finally letting me see his monster. *Show me yours and I'll show you mine.*

"All you bitches are asking for it," he snaps.

Rage.

Red. Carnal. Fucking. *RAGE.*

It sweeps over me before I can stop it. An inferno in my chest and my heart about to erupt out of it. I can't speak anymore so I grip the scalpel in my hand, shaking, and slash at the base of his pathetic cock.

He screams, a soothing sound.

Blood spurts from the raw opening. It coats the front of my dress, splattering all over me and the plastic sheeting on the floor.

"What about now?" I muse. "Am I still asking for it?"

The fucker is screaming at me now like I've actually cut it off. I haven't. It's still attached. With the right surgeon, and I'm sure he knows a few, he could stitch it back on. His eyes are white with terror. Obviously, shit-scared of losing his manhood more than anything else. I'm his worst nightmare come true.

Fuck the system.

I am the system.

I hum while he continues to cry, and I clean the metal of the scalpel on the material of my dress. There's blood everywhere. All over the bed. I didn't add any sheeting to the bed because he would have noticed it. I'll have to burn the sheeting and the mattress after this. That might be fun. I could have a little bonfire in the garden.

It's October, after all.

My favorite time of year.

"You fucking crazy bitch. Just you wait. You're fucking dead. Do you hear me? Dead!" He spits out his words.

I absolutely *hate* being called crazy.

Fucking paedo.

17

I slice the last of his dick off. The scalpel is sharp, so it hisses through flesh like a knife through warm butter. He's so loud, it's annoying. His bit of meat is still warm, bloody in my hands. I shove it into his open mouth to shut him up. He gags and tries to spit it out, to bite me, but I force it inside and take the square piece of electrical tape I prepared earlier and tape it over his mouth. Then I hack off his pair of pathetic-looking balls and plop them bloody onto the middle of his chest where he can see them.

He recoils, jerking against his bonds, blubbing with his streaming eyes, begging me to stop.

The fucker is crying actual tears.

They all beg in the end.

I clean the knife again and set it down neatly on the side table. I've done what I came to do. I've castrated him in the cruelest way possible. I don't have to do anything else.

I could let him bleed out, slowly, watch the light go out of his eyes as he finally gets it. Watch him choke on his own cock. He won't get a chance to make me suffer for what I've done. His threat is useless, empty. His life as he knows it is over. Even if he survives, he'll never be able to rape another little girl ever again.

Detached and almost dreamlike, I tilt my head for his last breaths. A feeling of euphoria envelopes my entire body. If I close my eyes and allow myself to drift off, I'll leave my body behind, seeing my life play out from afar. But why miss the best show on earth?

Eventually, he stops jerking and lies still. His eyes become like a doll's. Dead. Unseeing. The kind of eyes that pacify some erratic, wild part of me.

I climb off his body, no longer interested. I'm not a crazy killer, serial or otherwise. I don't take trophies or have rituals. I make sure of that. My job makes sure of that. Even if I've lost count of the bodies. Even if I need to feel *something*. I want nothing that can tie me to any murder.

The dead can't touch you. It's the living you have to watch out for.

TWO

VIOLA

I HAUL the bloody mattress and sheets out of the cabin, set the bonfire alight, and then take a long, cold, glorious fucking shower. There's no hot water in this dump, but I hate getting blood on my clothes just as much as I hate taking it back to my apartment. I take time to lather up. Letting the water beat my body until I'm shivering from the thrill just as much as the temperature.

Killing someone always gives me a heady rush. It leaves my body tingling, my mind reeling, and my heart racing.

And always wanting more.

It's an addiction. I know that. But what am I addicted to? What drives a person to kill over and over again? Is it an addiction for control, for power? If it is, I can't let it control me, no matter how much I revel in it. I can't lose my freedom. Not ever again. I need to let it go. I say this every time, but this is the last one. After this, no more.

I fucking promise.

After I'm clean, I make my way downstairs to check on the fire. I needn't have bothered. The flames are already devouring the evidence. I watch for a few seconds longer before turning back toward the house.

On the porch, I take out my burner phone and dial Dante's number. I know it off by heart. He's the only one who can help me clean up the rest of the mess tonight. I'm not strong enough to drag a dead body all the way downstairs and into the rear garden. In the past, before I knew Dante would help me, I used to cut the bodies up into pieces, so it was small enough to carry in sections. But I'm not in the mood to chop up body parts right now. It's messy and nasty.

Totally unnecessary.

Dante answers on the first ring. His words are devoid of emotion, straight up and direct.

"V? What's up?"

"Can I leave *it* here? I'll pay you to clean up."

There's a slight pause. "You know I'm working, don't you?"

"He's heavy," I say, being completely honest.

"There's a chainsaw in the garage."

"I don't want this to take hours. I have things to do tomorrow," I snap. I'm tired of this conversation already. "Look, I'll just leave *it* here? I'll even wrap a bow around it."

"Don't. I'm coming over."

"I thought you had work?"

There's a dial tone as Dante hangs up and not for the first time do I wonder if I've offended him. No. Dante couldn't give two fucks about helping me. He just likes being difficult. The added bonus of using his cabin for kills means he will make sure it's spotless.

I hate clean-up.

It's my least favorite part.

Dante on the other hand revels in it.

It's close to midnight when Dante arrives, driving his offensive brown Mustang, a car you'd struggle to see a mile down the road.

The car revs into the clearing. It has to be him. No one comes out here. No one actually knows this place exists except for me and Dante. The entrance is hidden from the road.

The peace I felt as the light left my prey's eyes has almost subsided. It never stays longer than a few hours now. My skin itches, my nerves are wrought, and my body vibrates as though it's truly alive. But I'm still the most serene I've felt in a long time. All the rage and emptiness within me has given way to a fragile calm. I cling to it like a lifeline.

Nothing in the world can ever hurt me, ever again.

Except getting caught.

Even if I clean up afterward, even if I'm careful, someone could trace it all back to me. No, not the police. I'm not scared of them. The system is broken. No. There are those who have more power than any law in the country or any country for that matter. They are the ones I need to steer clear of.

Thank fuck for fire. It burns away even the worst of my sins.

As soon as he parks up, he gets out, I leave the house and walk over to him. We don't make any kind of greeting. Dante's just not that type of person.

Tall, pale, with light blue eyes and blonde hair, he's all business and no play. His eyes are like two empty pools, dead and lifeless. It's like looking into the eyes of a shark. I've never seen him afraid or angry. Amused, yes, but never enough to make him appear human. I've no idea where Dante is from or how he came to be what he is. I just know I can trust him.

How? He saved my life once.

I owe him.

"You took your time," I say as soon as I reach him.

"Polina wanted to see me," he says as he looks up, spying the smoke from the fire. I know it's risky lighting one in the garden, but it is bonfire season. In less than a week, it'll be Halloween, and in ten days the 5th of November. Every garden in England will have a fire.

"Why?" Polina is Dante's contact. I've never met her, only

heard her voice when she calls me or us. She intrigues me, mainly because Dante jumps when she snaps her fingers.

"You didn't pick up or call her back."

"Is she pissed at me?" I ask, matter-of-factly.

Dante says nothing. Instead, he opens a pack of smokes, takes one out, and lights it. He takes a long drag, almost smoking the whole thing in one go before dropping the stub to the ground and putting it out. He then bends down to pick it back up reminding me we can't leave evidence anywhere, even in our own homes.

"Where's the body?" he finally asks.

"On the floor, wrapped in plastic sheeting, in the bedroom." I indicate with my head to the dilapidated house behind me that lies hidden from the rest of town behind the crest of Devil's hill. "Do you need help bringing it down?"

He gives me a sidelong look before shaking his head. "No, you'll just get in the way. Stay with the car. Call Polina back."

With that, he walks into the house. I suppress the urge to follow him. Dante knows where everything is.

He's right. He doesn't need my help and I *should* call Polina.

The Mustang isn't locked so I walk around to the passenger side and open the door.

Resting on the passenger seat is a plain manila folder. The kind that her agency's jobs come in. Polina must have given it to Dante on his way over here. I pick it up and get into the car then close and lock the door, before opening the file.

Inside the file is a photograph of a boy around my age, younger than me if his student uniform is anything to go by, looking into the camera with an arrogant smile, with messy, dark hair and intense green eyes. He's pretty too, if that's your type. I have a feeling I know him, although I've no idea where from.

A post-it note is stuck to the front of the boy's photograph and on it are scrawled details of what needs to be done to the head of London's most powerful crime family's son.

I read it three times, just to make sure I'm not seeing things.

What the hell kind of job is this?

24

I contemplate not calling her, but I know I need to. I'm just not in the mood to tell Polina why I took three hours to call her back. The longer I leave it the harder it's going to be. With a sigh, I call her latest cell. She doesn't answer on the first ring. She makes me wait. She's always making me wait.

Bitch.

"Polina, I'll take the job," I say before she can get a word out. There's no doubt in my mind, jobs like this don't come along often and pay very, very well.

"You're too late, Viola. I gave it to someone else."

Who, I wonder? "You know I'm the better choice or you wouldn't have asked me first."

"You don't even know what it is yet," she scoffs.

"I have it in front of me," I retort. "If it's for who I think it is, then you're going to need me." Dante isn't the type of person you put in front of normal people and expect them to feel safe. In fact, it's the total opposite.

"Then work with Dante on it. I honestly don't care."

And split the fee? That's a no. "I don't want to work with Dante. I can do this alone."

"And you think you have the finesse to do it?"

"Yes."

"Without Dante's help?"

"I get the job done *and* I make it look like an accident. What else is there?"

There's a long pause on the other end of the line. I can almost hear her breathing.

"Fine, it's yours. Don't fuck it up." She says it softly, enough that I have to really think about my next line. Polina is a person I don't want to fuck with.

"I won't."

"Goodbye, Viola." She hangs up.

A knock at the window has me looking up.

It's Dante wanting his car back. Behind him, the fire has kicked up a notch and the smoke has billowed out, turning black.

I stuff the job back in its file and unlock the Mustang door so Dante can slide into the driver's seat. His eyes brush over me and the file in my lap as he turns the engine. He smells of burnt things, cleaning chemicals, and cologne.

"Any trouble?" I ask.

"None." He starts the engine, looks behind him, and backs up. "All done. Was there a vehicle?"

"I left it in the garage."

He nods. "I'll deal with it later. Next time, no fires."

"Polina gave me the job," I say to distract him from a further lecture.

He blinks, glancing right at me for a second. "Oh?"

I ponder his reaction a moment, the rumble of the engine as we cruise along soothing me. "I can't imagine you'd have enjoyed it."

Dante doesn't work well with undercover-type jobs. Come to think of it, neither do I.

He contemplates. "You think you can do it alone?"

I look back out onto the road before us. It's pitch black as though we're traveling into the middle of hell, into the middle of nowhere.

I know what he's asking me.

Can I keep my rage under control? Can I do what they're asking me to without killing anyone else?

"I can do it."

Dante shrugs and stares at the horizon, not answering my question. "There's a package for you in the back seat."

I give him a look in askance but questioning Dante is like trying to get blood out of a stone. Reaching back between the seats of the Mustang, sure enough, a package is nestled on the leather there. I pull it through the gap between the seats and rest it on my lap. It's light and soft in my hands.

I open it up and stare at it, before holding the thin pleated strip of tartan aloft.

"You've got to be fucking kidding."

I glance at Dante. There's a slight curl to his lips at the edges. The bastard finds this amusing. He knew what this job would entail.

"I'll do the job but I'm not wearing a costume."

"That *is* the job. Protection and disposal. Double-edged sword."

I give him a look. I doubt Polina would ask Dante to stoop so low. Why do I feel like this is a set-up somehow?

"She wants me undercover, I get it. But enrolled? This has to be a joke; this isn't a real job. I am fucking twenty-three years old."

Dante says nothing but the smirk on his lips has grown bigger. The fucker is loving this. He parks up next to my car where I left it, opposite the bar where I stalked my prey earlier in the night.

I hold up the pleated burgundy and purple tartan skirt and stare at it. This job had better be worth it. The photograph on my lap seems to taunt me.

There's only one problem.

I *do* know this boy.

And that's never good when you have to pretend to be someone you're not.

THREE

VIOLA

WHAT THE HELL *do I look like?*

As soon as I saw the awful school uniform Polina sent me, my first thought was hell no. But I go ahead and strip to my panties and bra, trying it on as soon as I walk through the door to my apartment, anyway.

The white shirt clings to my modest breasts. I'm thankful for the sweater and blazer, giving me some coverage. But the pleated skirt is really fucking short. *Like, really short.*

Never in my life have I worn a school uniform like this. There wasn't even a dress code, never mind a uniform, at the shitty school my caseworker forced me to attend. Ironic, really, that I despised school, and now here I am wearing the most atrocious thing I've ever put on my body, about to go back to the place that represents where my nightmares started.

Only this time you're not vulnerable anymore, Viola.

Fuck that. Who cares. I'm twenty-three, not seventeen.

I can't do this.

I close my eyes and open them again, taking another look at myself. *Wearing this, I could pass for a schoolgirl. I have a very* young-looking babyface. Polina once told me that my mixed ethnicity and innocent looks gave me an advantage in life. Well. I'm paraphrasing. Her exact words were… "You're every man's wet dream. An exotic Lolita any guy is going to want hanging off his cock."

I'm not sure I agree with her, but if it keeps me on her payroll, I don't really care. Her words and opinions mean nothing to me. And if it gets me the best jobs, the ones I'm suited to, the ones with assholes who need to be taught a lesson, then so be it.

Polina is right. I have no choice. If I want to kill my target without getting caught, I need to blend in around his school. It's where he spends most of his time. I need to stalk him all the fucking time. It's the only way to plan his demise effectively.

On the side table are the rest of the files Polina sent me after accepting the job. More photographs and more bedtime reading.

I open the top folder, the one pertaining to the victim, and remove the photo of the girl with light brown hair and piercing blue eyes. She's sweet-looking in a way that I could have been if I hadn't had the life I did.

I already decided my approach is going to be simple. I know what I am, what I look like. My looks are the draw here. Killing for fun is messy, chaotic. But killing for work needs to be controlled. I need to do this right, but that doesn't mean it can't be entertaining.

And looking like the bastard's last victim is highly entertaining in my book.

In my vanity are several wigs and colored lenses. I pick a pair of blue lenses and a wig that matches the color and hairstyle of the girl in the photo. It doesn't need to be identical, just similar. It's a case of becoming a lamb, but not too much of one. I don't want to be eaten by wolves… I just want to lure one to his death.

I wash my hands and pop a lens into each eye, blinking several times to get them to settle. Then, I bend over from the waist so that my long blonde hair falls forward and I shove it under the auburn wig.

Fluffing my new hair into some kind of style that goes with the innocent look, I angle my head at my reflection in the mirror. Compared to the picture of the girl, I could pass for her sister.

Polina, you bitch. You knew that when you hired me.

And the uniform...

I turn around so I can see what the skirt looks like from the rear. The pleats make it bounce on my ass, and if I bend over slightly... there, you can see my fucking knickers.

Right.

There's no fucking way I'm wearing this.

I end up wearing it—a modified version of the school uniform with shorts beneath the skirt, and one of my white shirts that hasn't been starched into cardboard. I combine the look with the lightest touches of makeup and poker-straight hair. No heels. I prefer boots.

On the drive in from my rented house, I listen to my *Violent Tendencies* playlist and study the paperwork the school sent me, and the schedules of all the students I need to know about. I also go over Polina's files again. There are three files in total—one for the victim so I can get a sense of the killer's type, one on the client so I can understand who we're working for, and one with everything known about the killer. I like to go over the files and the evidence, and imprint the brutality of it all in my mind so it's fresh for the first day on the job.

It helps me to get in the mood.

I finish reading by the time we get to Sacré-Cœur Preparatory School in West London. Turning off into a winding driveway through parklands, leading up to a grand edifice built from gray stone and pewter slate, the chained up, 20ft high, black twisted metal gates remind me of everything I hate about this country's elite education system. I've never even heard of this place before today.

Thankfully, Polina's files have a brief history of the institution.

Sacré-Cœur Prep, or Sacred Heart to its students, is a school notorious for its unique patronage—an elite academy rife with the offspring of so many mafia families, it's become a training ground for the next generation of organized crime. In fact, there are more unsolved murder cases per year in the towns surrounding Sacred Heart than there are mafia families attending the school itself, and there are a lot.

As if to drive home the danger about the place, outside the drop-off area there's a checkpoint. Security men study my credentials against the list and search my car, a rented Bentley for show, and then wave us through.

Finally, we pull into a large courtyard where a dried-up fountain sits squat in the middle, and park at the curb.

I check myself in the mirror before sliding out of the back seat and into daylight.

Another chauffeur-driven car appears in the driveway as I start up the stone steps. It parks up. Loud, classical music blasts from inside as the rear passenger door flies open. A school kid, taller and broader than me in every way, with a deadpan expression, gets out ignoring whatever the other passenger is saying to him.

"Lorcan, don't ignore me—"

He slams the door, cutting off their words.

He may be a schoolboy, but he's tall and broad and looks ready to rip out of that white shirt, which is only half-buttoned up. Dark hair mussed, blazer slung over shoulder, he takes the steps two at a time.

He adjusts his headphones, heavy metal blasting out of them, and glances up the steps to where I'm standing. His green eyes meet mine. He frowns back as soon as he sees me, like my very existence hurts. Slowly he blinks, the confusion in his eyes fading away until he's almost nonchalant in his observation of me.

The passenger in the car that dropped him off called him Lorcan.

Lorcan Duke.

As always, my timing is impeccable.

He looks older and less innocent-looking than his picture in the file. It makes me wonder how up to date those photographs are that Polina sent me, and if I might need better intel on the eldest heir of one of the most powerful crime families this side of the Atlantic.

As if sensing my interest, Duke flicks his cold gaze to me as he passes by. A lightness fills my chest, and my pulse quickens. I appraise him with a cool look in return until his brow furrows and he shakes his head, disappearing up the steps and into the dark building.

He doesn't look back.

Inside the school is not as pretty or as perfect as outside. Wide corridors and vaulted ceilings greet me once through the main entrance. The place would seem regal if it were not for the cracked wall, dented lockers, and scuffed floors, on top of the stale smell of rot and chalk dust clouding the air. Even the privileged kids with their designer accessories, immaculate hair, and polished shoes appear fraught and uncomfortable.

Duke is nowhere to be seen, despite having entered seconds before me. Not that I want to catch up to him just yet. I need to get my bearings. I need to work this place out so I know all the exits and dark spots, and just who might be lurking around every corner.

There's another security check. I pass through it with flying colors despite the five-inch dagger strapped higher than usual to my thigh under the short skirt. I almost want them to pat me down.

Once my bags have been given the all clear, I take a left and push through the throng of kids towards the main office following the signs. The halls are teeming with adolescents gossiping and goofing off. Every so often one of them brushes against me. I bury the urge to hurt someone so far down that I don't know what the fuck I'm doing until I get into the empty walkway and I can breathe.

I fucking hate crowds, I hate being touched, and I hate school kids. This place is my worst nightmare come true. Somewhere, Dante is pissing himself laughing right this very moment. *He won't find it funny when I fuck some kid up, and he has to come and clean up the mess.*

I reach the registration office just as another *fucking* schoolboy—they are everywhere—is coming out of it. Tall, looking much older than eighteen, with red hair and striking blue eyes. He grins at me and holds open the door, effectively blocking it, like he expects me to squeeze through the gap under his arm. *Like hell, I'm doing that.*

I come to a halt in front of him.

His eyes move up and down, taking me in. "Well, this place just keeps getting better and better."

"Move," I say calmly.

He narrows his eyes at me. "Have we met? I feel like I've seen you before."

"I seriously doubt it. Are you going to move, or do I have to make you?"

"Bossy little thing, aren't you?" He smirks. "You must be new. What's your name?"

"You have three seconds to move before I break something." Only ten minutes in and this place is already getting to me. *Not good.*

At that, his eyes practically dance with excitement. "Feisty. I like it. Nice to meet you, new girl who won't be named."

Retracting his arm from the door, slowly, he moves past. He flicks the end of my hair as he does. I don't react but the intense burning feeling I've come to associate with extreme violence settles over me like a fog.

This boy is lucky I don't snap his fucking fingers one by one.

I count to ten and wait until he's gone and the buzzing under my skin has faded, before approaching the registrar's desk. I school my expression into one that doesn't look like I want to kill someone as she looks up at me. Still, the registrar pales and does a double-take as soon as she sees me.

"Aurora?"

"No. Victoria. Victoria Hartridge," I repeat. "I'm transferring to Sacred Heart today?"

I wait for her to regain her composure before handing her my papers. "Oh my, I thought you were a ghost for a minute there." She takes my papers, looking them over, glancing at me every so often. "Yes, yes, of course. This looks to be everything I need. I just have to add you to the system. This may take a few moments."

I never doubted for one second the papers wouldn't be legit. Quinn, my ex, can get me in anywhere. She's the reason I got into this school so quickly. And after I'm done...

She'll be my way out of it.

The tapping of her keyboard and the whirl of the fan are the only sounds as I wait. I don't bother to make small talk until she probes me for more information. "It's so unusual to have a student start late in the final year," the registrar says as she types. "Did you just move here or..."

"My mother travels around a lot for business," I say.

"Not your father?" she asks, bobbing her head as she looks between the papers and the monitor.

I can't help but give her a blank look.

When I don't answer, the registrar's face softens, sympathetic indicators reaching her eyes. I draw the line at having a father, even a make-believe one, but that's my business and no one else's.

Prying bitch.

She hands me my welcome pack and I plaster on a fake smile because I'm meant to be blending in, just as a gust of wind blows in through the door as it opens behind me.

The registrar's face brightens as she sees who it is. "Ah, Carly, my dear. What brings you here?"

"Mrs. Waterford sent me," a girlish voice says. I turn around.

Dark brown eyes stare at me from under a brunette pixie cut. I immediately recognize the girl from the student roster—Carlotta Earlshore, one of the top performing arts students at Sacred Heart with international fame, whose family is well known for shady dealings in rare and expensive antiquities. She's carrying an antique trombone case laden with tourist stickers as if to drill home that fact.

"Victoria? I'm here to show you around campus."

Earlshore turns and exits the office before I have a chance to answer.

When I get outside, she's waiting for me, tapping her foot, a permanent scowl on her face. I took my sweet time gathering my papers and books. It makes me happy to see her frothing at the mouth at how long I made her wait.

"Hartridge. I've not heard of your family. What do they do again?"

"My mother's a lawyer," I say, keeping it vague.

She sniffs. Obviously, that wasn't the answer she was hoping for. "Well, I would give you the grand tour, but I have music practice so… this is a map of the school. That's the library. Classrooms are here and here. Food hall for lunch and dinner. This is where the science labs are and next to it is the campus store. And that tall building behind you, the one with the narrow windows, is the music block." She says it all in one breath, pointing to all parts of the map before she shoves it at me.

You're not getting away that easy. "The handbook mentioned a common room."

"Oh, that place. It's next to the library, but it's permanently closed," she says.

"Closed?"

She gives me a narrowed look. "You know about the murder, right?"

I do, but I want to hear first hand. I screw my face up pretending to look worried. "I saw something on the news about suicides. It happened recently, right?"

Carly glances at her watch, before giving in to the delight behind her eyes. She's loving this. "Last week. Everyone's still in shock. Killing yourself for attention is one thing, but being brutally murdered..." She shudders.

"I thought the police haven't ruled it out as being suicide yet?"

Carly shakes her head. "There's no way it was suicide. I was the one who found her. She was a mess. Blood everywhere. They say she stabbed herself five times."

"Stabbed? I thought she hung herself?" The news report didn't mention the state of her body, but the file I have is full to the brim with photos of the crime scene. She'd been beaten, raped, and then gutted. Someone is paying a lot of money to cover this up, hence me being hired in the first place.

Interesting that whoever is pulling the police strings couldn't keep the students quiet too. Earlshore doesn't have a fucking clue how much danger she could be in by telling me all this.

Carly shrugs. "The school is trying to keep it hush-hush. I expect that's why the police haven't released all the details."

"Do they have any idea who did it?"

"There's talk it could be anyone. Someone from this school even."

She closes her eyes briefly, making her shoulders quiver. A single tear leaks from under her lashes. "She was in my class. Finding her like that..." Her voice breaks.

I show the appropriate amount of concern. "How awful for you." For a top performing arts student, Carly Earlshore is a shit actress.

Carly nods her head and sighs, eventually looking up to stare right at me. Her brow creasing. "You know, you look just like her."

"Like the dead girl?"

"Sorry. That's probably not what you want to hear." She glances down at her watch. "Shit, I'm late. I have to go."

"Wait. If there's no common room, where do the students hang out?"

She shrugs. "The library? Or we go to the old boathouse sometimes," she says. She points to a solo building, next to the lake on the map.

I arch a brow at her. "Seems far from campus. Don't the staff mind students hanging out there unsupervised after what happened?"

"We go in groups. The staff are too afraid to stop us."

"Us?"

She gives me a pitiful look, as though I don't know anything. "You must have heard of the five founding families who own this school?"

I make a mental note to ask Quinn to send me everything on the founders, all five of them. "I haven't actually."

She tilts her head, eyes narrowed. Finally, she speaks. "The Dukes throw wild parties sometimes, if you're into that sort of thing?"

I cock my brow at the word 'wild'. "Sure," I say, feeling the buzz under my skin for the first time since I got here.

She smiles. "Great. Ask one of Duke's boys, they'll add you to the list."

After she's gone, I check the map to see where the common room is, and then walk the long way around to avoid any of the staff. I want to see the scene with my own eyes.

They say killers always go back to the scene of the crime.

How easy would my job be if he was there?

38

FOUR

DINO

FUCK BEING BACK AT SCHOOL. I push through the outer doors and head to where there aren't any cameras, pull out my smokes, and light one. There's a message from Kristian. I read it and then pocket my phone, not bothering to reply. It's about our mother. Stupid bitch has gone into rehab again. Like I give a fuck.

Inhale hard. And then let it out.

I take another drag, letting the ash burn my fingers as I take it all the way to the stub. Fuck that's good. It's the only thing making me feel alive.

My phone buzzes again. I scowl and breathe out a lungful of hot air, then yank my phone out.

Come straight home after school. We need to talk.

I highly doubt my brother wants to talk about the bitch who gave birth to us. He wants me involved. *That ain't fucking happening.*

I type out a reply and hit send.

Nothing to talk about.

I clench my jaw and switch my phone off before he calls. I don't want to talk to Kristian. Apart from my throat feeling like it's about to close up, I have enough shit to worry about. Like the fucking drug test the officials made me take. It wasn't random. I know that. Just like I knew it was always going to come back positive and get me fucking kicked off the race team. I worked so hard to get on that fucking team. Someone set me up.

Saskia.

I bet it was her fucking father.

He thinks I'm not good enough for his fucking ice princess. Who gives a fuck? He can keep her. The Dukes deserve each other. All three of them deserve each other.

I take another drag, running my hand through my hair, looking up as someone catches my eye.

The new girl enters the quad. She's staring straight ahead with that stony glare of hers. I've been around enough sharks to know one when I see one.

Who is she? Which family owns her pert little ass?

Carly texted me just before Kristian did. She wants me to take the new girl to Duke's next party—fuck that. I'll go alone. It's not like I can race anytime soon so I may as well get shit-faced like the rest, but I'm not bringing anyone. Lorcan's parties make me sick to my stomach. I understand why he has them. They're a necessary evil. But hell, I draw the line at delivering girls to him who have no fucking clue what they're getting themselves into.

If the new girl wants to go, and most girls do when they're invited, I'll tell her what the deal is. For no other reason other than I think she deserves a chance before the wolves eat her for breakfast.

I watch her from my hidden spot behind the roses as she walks quickly across the quad, toward the old common room and away from the main building where classes are held, books clasped in her arms. The common room is closed. Surely, someone told her that. *What the hell are you up to, new girl?* She looks so innocent, but after our run-in at reception, I know it's an act. Everyone here is putting on a front, why should she be any different?

A moment later that perverted fucking history teacher, Prof. Barnsley, enters the quad following after her.

Unease gnaws in the pit of my stomach.

I take another drag.

Fuck it.

I grind the stub out and drop it into the flower bed where hundreds of the things litter the ground, and then grab my blazer tossed over the low wall. I'm gasping for another one, but my vape will have to do.

I should follow her. Just in case she gets into trouble. I'm supposed to be in class, but I don't give a toss. No one in this school would say a word. My dad would fuck anyone up who suggested I might not be welcome here.

As long as the five own this school, I'm going fucking nowhere.

FIVE

VIOLA

THE COMMON ROOM is indeed closed when I get there. Yellow and black tape zigzags across the doorway like a bad omen.

I duck beneath it and try the door. It's not locked so it swings open, assaulting my senses with the stench of death and body odor. I do a quick scan of the room, making sure I'm alone and then I do my own sweep for clues.

Even though my client knows who did it, I still like to have all the facts. Not because I won't do the job. I'm not a fucking saint. But because if my target didn't do this... *I want to know who did.*

The room is ice cold compared to the rest of the school, and my breath fogs in the air as I move around the scene. I note anything and everything that appears related to the crime—a blood mark on the wall, a dubious smear on the glass window.

In the middle of the room, beneath the central supporting beam, is a large brown stain dried into the carpet. It's where she bled to death. The killer hung her up on the beam to drain her body of fluid, exactly like you would a farm animal post-slaughter.

He didn't give a fuck about her. She was chattel to him.

The red mist I try to carefully keep under wraps is starting to unravel, so I work quickly. Unclenching my hands, I pull out my phone and snap the stain, and then take pictures of the smears on the walls and glass. It's odd there are no splatter marks. If she was beaten, raped, and stabbed, it wasn't here.

I'm just finishing up when the entrance cranks open. The edgy, twitchy feeling ramps up tenfold.

"You're not supposed to be in here." A middle-aged man in a brown jacket and a very bad receding hairline says as he sees me. "Shouldn't you be in class?"

I school my face into an innocent expression and force my body to relax, casually dropping my phone into my pocket. "It's my first day. I think I'm lost."

His eyes narrow. "Okay, well this place is off-limits. It's an active crime scene. Miss…?"

He must be a teacher. There's no way I'm giving him my name, even if it is fake. I shift my stance, so my hip is cocked, angling my head as I pull the map out Carly gave me.

"Can you help me?" I ask, looking at him coyly from under my lashes.

He nods. Desire, as I knew it would, flares in the depths of his lecherous gaze as he watches me unfold the map.

"I'm supposed to be in history right now, sir, can you show me outside where the Juliet building is?" I say, walking towards him.

Instead of waiting for me to get to him, he takes a step forward and then another, closing the door behind him. His eyes are dark, almost shining as they take me in.

Okay.

I pegged him completely wrong. *Fucking horny bastard.*

Time to leave.

Blinking my eyes a few times, I breathe in and out, so it looks as though I'm about to hyperventilate.

"Are you okay?"

I shake my head. "I feel a bit faint, sir. It must be all the blood. I need to go outside and get some air," I lie.

His brow furrows. "You… don't look well."

"I think I'm going to throw up." I put my hand over my mouth for effect.

He pales, just like I knew he would, and stops, unsure what to do. I don't waste time. I quickly walk past him, ignoring how close he is, and push through the gap. I don't stop moving until I'm in broad daylight.

Unfortunately, he follows me. "Wait, I haven't finished with you yet," he says. His hand on my arm drags me back. Outside I'm calm, inside I'm fucking screaming.

It takes me only seconds to react.

I spin around, senses heightened, heart thundering, eyes slitted and full of malice. *I'm going to gouge your eyes out for even thinking you can touch me.*

He frowns.

And fortunately for him, a baritone voice cuts through the crazy. "I'd take my hands off her if I was you."

Startled, the teacher releases his grip on me. *Do that again, and I'll make it really hurt.* I blink sharply a few times and look left. We both do.

It's the tall, undeniably sexy redhead who barred my way into reception. He's leaning against the brick wall of the common room exterior, partially hidden behind clumps of roses, vaping and texting on his phone. Blazer on the floor, tie askew like he's recently yanked at it, sleeves rolled up to expose scars down both muscled forearms—he looks like no teenager I've ever met.

The teacher narrows his eyes and shifts in his stance, trying to make himself bigger. It's no use, he's scrawnier than the red head. "Oh, Vice, it's you. I thought you were suspended?"

"Professor Barnsley, you know my dear ol' dad threatened to burn this dump to the ground if your boss didn't let me in sooner," he says with a glint in his eye, taking another inhale of his vape.

Barnsley. So that's who you are.
You're now on my list.

Barnsley snorts, coughing a little as the smoke from Vice's vape—liquorice flavor from the smell—billows toward us. "I see. Well, I guarantee you'll be suspended again within a week."

"Now why would I do that and miss all this fun?" Vice takes another long drag of his vape, and squints against the glaring sunlight as he looks at me. "You alright? Need an escort to class?"

"No. I'm fine," I say. And I am. A few deep breaths of liquorice-flavored smoke seems to have soothed the ragged edges inside my soul. If I even have a soul.

But I didn't need rescuing. And I don't have time for drama. I should be back in class stalking my prey.

"If you're not suspended, shouldn't you be in class? Do I need to write you both up for detention?"

"I was on my way to class, sir," I say through gritted teeth.

"Then go, now, before I change my mind."

Vice opens his mouth. Before he can say anything, I give him an unfiltered, shitty look, one that says back-the-fuck-off, and turn around, walking away from the beginnings of a male cock fight towards the main building.

If the teacher had tried anything, and Vice hadn't been there, I would have blown my cover, so for that I'm slightly thankful. Not that I'll ever admit it out loud.

You're not here to kill mother-fucking paedo teachers. You're here for a job—a paying one.

I glance back at the teacher, burning his ferret-like face into the recesses of my mind. I never forget a face.

Because this one only gets a free pass… *for now.*

It takes some engineering to get a seat on the desk next to my target. All I have to do is angle my gaze left and a polished, aquiline profile and a swathe of dark hair comes into view.

He's older. Not a scrawny kid anymore.

Well, it has been three years since I saw him last.

The first time was outside his father's office, before I worked for Polina. I used to take smaller 'seduction' type jobs from her rivals. This guy wasn't a target then. Hell, *he* wasn't even on my watchlist. He was just the son of some super rich, crime lord asshole who wanted me to honeytrap an employee blackmailing the family business.

While I sat in the reception area waiting to see his father, *he* was sitting opposite. Quiet, composed, and disinterested in me. That never happens.

But I noticed him.

I observed him when my client came out to greet me. The look he gave his father was far from pleasant.

It was downright evil.

The second time we met, his father hired me to find and retrieve him from a junkie-infested penthouse apartment in Hackney. It was over three years ago. As dark as it was inside that house, I recognized the same pretty boy despite being fucked up on whatever it was he'd shoved up his nose.

Question is, does he remember me?

Just like on the stone steps, my target shifts in his position as if suddenly aware of my attention. He looks right at me. Green eyes like shattered glass latch onto mine, regarding me with a callous gaze.

It's a look I've seen before...many times in the mirror. Dismissive, dark, lacking anything deep or emotive. I stare back, unflinching, letting him see the part of me I constantly have to hide.

The ugly part.

The part that's not pretty.

His eyes narrow but the intrigue is real.

It takes a lot to break away, go back to my textbooks like nothing else matters in the world. The urge to observe some more, study *him* in every way, is suffocating. The dark void inside me is awake and wanting...

But that's enough for now. A brief connection is all I need.

I don't look at Duke again throughout the class, but I catch him watching me out of the corner of my eye. He can't not look. I'm pretty and new, and there's something familiar about me he won't be able to work out.

As class finishes, I gather my things and Duke comes straight over.

"Do I know you?" The intensity of the way he looks at me could burn this place to the ground, turning it into smoldering ash.

"No."

His brow furrows as he opens his mouth to say something else, eyes full of self-importance, but I disregard him and turn away.

"Wait, I wasn't done—"

I walk until I'm out of class. I sense him following me, but I keep moving quickly until I get too far down the hallway. At the last minute, I look over my shoulder to see him standing at the other end of the hall. The furrow in his brow hasn't gone away. The expression on his pretty face is arrogant and unpleasant. He's a guy used to getting what he wants. I bet he didn't like chasing after me like that.

Tough shit. I'm not acting like other girls. I'm not *like* other girls. And I'm good at getting under a guy's skin, especially ones who like to break seemingly innocent, sweet young girls like me.

And now, he knows it too.

Before lunch, I stop to open my locker, or I would if the redhead from the morning wasn't lounging against it with a flirtatious look on his face.

He smirks, lips full and teasing. "Feisty girl, we meet again. We got off on the wrong foot earlier. Fancy a do-over?" he says, voice as smooth as silk.

"Ignore him. He just wants to get in your pants. Vice here will sleep with anything with a heartbeat," says a girl with long, raven hair, wearing a pair of dark shades. She comes over to where we're standing and gives me a once-over. "So, you're the new girl everyone's having an orgasm about?"

"Vickie, meet Saskia Duke, our resident Great White," the guy grins at me, teeth flashing. "Did you walk into a door again, Sassy?"

Duke. My target's sister.

I glance at the raven-haired girl with new eyes. I should have recognized her. I would have done if it wasn't for the designer dark glasses hiding not a thing.

Saskia's mouth flattens into a thin line. "Go fuck yourself, Vice."

"I would if I could," he taunts. "Seriously though, Sas, what the fuck happened?" His tone softens ever so slightly.

"Nothing happened."

"You did that to yourself then, did you?"

"I'm not here for your pity," she scoffs. "I came to see what all the fuss is about."

She turns her attention on me. "And, honestly, I don't see it."

"Like I give a fuck," I say as I turn back to my locker.

Vice, as he seems to be known as, snorts a laugh.

Beneath her shades, Saskia scowls. "Since you're obviously new and stupid, I'll give you a pass this time. A word of advice though, stay in your lane, Vickie." She plasters a snide smile onto her face and stalks off down the hallway.

A few paces down, she whips the glasses off and stuffs them in her blazer pocket. Even in the low light of the school hallway, you can clearly see the black eye, no matter how much concealer the girl has tried to cake on.

The redhead rolls his eyes. "Ignore her, she's a grade-A bitch. She's just upset because you were eye-fucking her brother in class."

"I don't give a fuck who she is," I say, grabbing the books I need. I close my locker and then give him a direct look. "You didn't know my name earlier."

He flashes the screen of his phone. "There's an article about you in the school rag, Vic-Tory-Ah. Interesting read. Says absolutely fuck all, if I'm honest. Where's your accent from again?"

Quinn needs to take that fucking article down.

"Are you always this nosy?" I put back to him, ignoring the question.

"You don't know the half of it," he says, lips curling up into a smirk.

I give him a deadpan look before turning away, heading toward the main lobby. He follows me like a goddamn puppy.

"So, Vic-Tory-Ah. Can I escort you to lunch?" The look he gives me is hopeful.

Saskia and the teacher earlier called him *Vice*.

The Vices are reputed to be one of the nastiest drug dealing families to ever grace London. It's hard to imagine this cocky, over-eager spaniel as anything but a GQ cover model. He must be a friend of Duke's since he's clearly one of the five, although I've yet to see them around school campus together. If the gossip is true, he's also Saskia's ex. It might be worth hanging around with him. He could have dirt on them both worth knowing.

I adjust my bag's shoulder strap, so it doesn't dig in. "I don't even know your name."

"Kardinal Vice at your fucking service. But you can call me Dino." The wink he gives me is too fucking cute. "So is that a yes?"

"Fine."

I'm not calling you fucking Dino.

He offers me his arm, but I don't take it. I'm able to walk just fine on my own. It's only when I see my target watching me as I enter the cafeteria that I lock my jaw and sidle a little closer to Vice.

It gets me noticed…

Even though the cafeteria is buzzing, my target, sitting like a kingpin among his so-called loyal friends, tosses a casual glower my way. A lock of hair has fallen over his eyes, softening the harshness of his gaze.

It's obvious to everyone in the room he's watching me. Others around him glance over to see what the fuss is about.

After we pick up our lunch trays, I follow Vice to an empty table, toward the far end. Not the table I was hoping for, but I'll take it. I sit with my back to the wall. From where I'm seated, I have a full view of the whole room….and my target.

Not that I'm looking at him directly. I'm giving Vice my full attention. I can turn on the charm when I want to. All I have to do is maintain eye contact and smile as Vice talks about himself. Eventually, the inevitable happens.

Duke gets up and comes over to where we're sitting. He leans forward on the back of the chair next to Vice. "You're winding my sister up, dickhead," he drawls at him.

"She broke up with me, Lorcan. I'm not playing the fucking saint for her ego any longer." Vice says, giving him a pointed stare.

"Don't fuck about, you're just hoping this cunt will let you get your dick wet."

"Charming," I sigh, picking up my juice box and jamming the pointed end of the straw through the sealed hole. *I hate that word.*

Lorcan looks up at me, our eyes colliding across the table.

I don't turn away this time. I stare right back, drinking my juice.

You have to give them a little something.

Breadcrumbs.

Outwardly, I'm calm. Inwardly, my heart beats rapidly like the wings of a bird caught in flight. Not out of fear. Out of excitement. It's like he knows who I am and why I'm here. It's like he's been waiting for me his whole life.

He probably has.

"I know you," he says, in that cold, arrogant way of his.

"No. I don't think so," I say, putting my drink down. My tone is a little colder than I intend.

A flare of something sparks deep within his icy emerald eyes as he narrows them. "No, I do. I *know* you from somewhere. What's your name, sweetheart?"

None of your fucking business.

I wet my lips and cock my head. "Victoria," I say, forcing it out. It's hard work pretending all day, but right now I can't let it slip. Duke needs to see the mask. Not the demon behind it. Not until it's too fucking late.

His eyes narrow as he gives me the once over. "Victoria. You don't look like a Victoria. What's your last name?"

"It's Hartridge. There's an article about her family on the school website," says Vice, a little too helpfully.

I shoot the most annoying redhead I've ever known a shitty fake smile. The spaniel has a big mouth, I must remember that.

"Hartridge. Never heard of it," drawls Lorcan. He hasn't taken his eyes off me the entire time. The corner of his mouth pulls up into a sultry, half smile.

"It's been my name my whole life." The lie eases off my tongue like honey. But it's not enough.

He remembers something.

"Duke," I say when I get within earshot of my 'package' doing a line of coke in the kitchen, with a Sloaney-type girl half-cut and hanging off him.

The rich brat looks up. As soon as he sees me, he cocks his head and frowns. I'm not expecting him to be tall or devilishly pretty. Dark hair, full lips, snarl permanently etched on his face, tattoos. You know the type —he's going to be a fucking drop-dead gorgeous asshole when he's older.

"Who the fuck are you?" His English accent is clipped as he takes me in.

"A friend," I say.

He eye-fucks me up and down, taking in my big hoop earrings, cherry red lips, ultra-tight hot pants and plunging halter neck top. To get an invite to this place all I had to do was dress like the common call girl. East London has them in spades if you know what phone booth to visit.

He snorts. "Hot, but I don't fuck gold-digging bitches. Now piss off, I'm busy."

When I don't leave, the girl clinging to his waist sneers. "Fucking trash, you heard what Duke said. Fuck off, who knows what kind of diseases you have."

"Will you shut the hell up, Tansy," he scowls.

"I'm not here to fuck. Just here to take you home," I say in a level voice.

Green eyes, dilated to the max, vivid even in this light, harden as he looks at me again. He lets out a lungful of air. "Another bodyguard? You've got to be fucking kidding me. Tell my father to go screw himself. I'm done. Tell him to find another fucking puppet. And no offense, but I could throw you over my shoulder." He shakes his head at me like I'm dismissed, and then bends over to snort the last of the blow off the countertop.

Little fucking shit. I could knock him out. But then there's no way I'd be able to carry him home if I do.

Still, I love it when they underestimate me.

"Duke."

He looks up. "Didn't you fucking hear me? I said piss off."

"Say cheese," I take out my phone and snap him with a line of white dust all over his face.

"What the fuck. Bitch!" hisses Tansy. "Lorcan, do something. She's going to post it online."

"What the fuck are you doing?" he snaps, shoving a hysterical Tansy away from him. He gets right in my face, doing a bang-up job of appearing sober when he's so fucking not. As he moves to grab my arm, I slam the heel of my hand into his chin making him stumble back.

The open Krug bottle on the granite worktop falls over. Golden liquid spills everywhere. He releases me in two seconds flat. "Bitch, do you know how much these shoes cost—"

He doesn't get to say another word because I've taken hold of his arm and twisted it around behind him, shoving him into the cold granite so *his face is kissing the wet surface. I did turn his head at the last minute to avoid breaking his nose. I doubt my employer would be happy if I smashed their son's face in.*

I would be though.

I was fine until he touched me. The little shit. Thought he could put his hands all over me. No one has that right.

"No more fucking games. I'm tired and cranky. It's been a long night." Not to mention this is the third drugged-up house party I've been to tonight just looking for this little bastard.

"You fucking cunt." Duke snarls into the puddle of alcohol I'm pushing him down into. He struggles in my grasp and it's like trying to keep a wild bull from stampeding.

"Don't call me that again or try to move, or I'll break both your arms and use them to drag you out of here. I'm telling you now, that will bloody fucking hurt. Do you understand?"

"What's wrong with you? Are you a fucking psycho or something?!"

Wrong answer.

I dislocate his arm instead of breaking it. The popping noise and his scream is drowned out by the beat of the music. I use the opportunity to yank his ass off the counter and drag him to his feet. He's taller than me by at least a foot. I unsheathe the blade I keep strapped to my thigh and poke it against his ribs.

"You fucking broke my arm!"

"I dislocated it. If you're a good boy, I'll pop it back in. Now fucking move, or I'll stab you in the groin, which would be a shame. I hear you're a decent cricket player." I'm not joking. I'll cripple him faster than he can blink.

I didn't cripple him, but I hurt teenage Lorcan Duke a lot, dragging him all the way down from that penthouse apartment while Tansy screamed at me until I broke her nose. No one else fucking batted an eyelid after that. Needless to say, after I delivered my package back to his father, I never saw Lorcan Duke again.

Until now.

Do you remember that night, or do I remind you of a dead girl?

Whatever he sees in my face, he keeps it to himself.

"Do you know who I am?" Lorcan asks instead, face unreadable.

I shrug. "Nope."

My unassuming reaction makes the muscle in his jaw clench.

He drags his gaze back to Vice. "Bit of a step down after my sister, isn't she?" His tone is flat and guarded despite the insult.

"Fuck your sister," Vice retorts.

Lorcan moves fast. He yanks Vice up by his half-knotted tie, dragging him out of the chair as it topples backwards, and shoves him down onto the table.

Everything lurches sideways. I calmly grab my tray and elevate it from the table as it shifts under the weight of the boys. I'm hungry. I'm not going to lose my lunch.

"Lorcan! Don't." A girl screeches from across the room. It's Saskia.

Lorcan hesitates, glaring at Vice. Finally, he lets him go. Breathing hard, he gives me one last look, and then drops Vice like a sack of potatoes. He strides away, back to where his sister is staring at me as though this is all my fault, open-mouthed, as vicious-looking as a mother viper in a nest of baby snakes.

Duke can't help himself though. His eyes seek me out as soon as he gets back to his seat. He's frowning hard, trying to work me out.

That's the kid I pulled from the penthouse?

I stare him down.

Do you remember Aurora and what you did to her? You gutted her like a pig. And I'm going to do the same to you. I would never say any of that out loud... not until he's strapped to my table and I can show him personally all the ways he fucked up.

SIX

LORCAN

I KNOW HER. I fucking *know* her.

For the life of me, I can't remember where from. *Did I fuck her, or is she one of those rich bitches my father's always parading in my face?*

He's always trying to get me to seduce the whore offspring of some cocksucker so he can negotiate a better deal. I'm expected to fuck them, drop them, and then move onto the next. It's fucking exhausting. It's no wonder I don't remember.

Back in my seat across the cafeteria, I can't keep my eyes off her. I don't know why. There's something about her that draws me in. She definitely reminds me of someone.

Saskia catches me staring. "Is she that special?"

"What?"

She frowns. "You're totally oblivious. Finn just asked you a question."

"Lor, mate. You're away with the fucking fairies," Finn adds.

Saskia clouts me around the back of the head.

"What the fuck is that for?" I say to my sister, ignoring Finn.

"That's for Dino."

"The fucker is fine."

"I *dumped* him."

"Since you're not eating." Finn reaches over and scoops a handful of fries off my plate. I glare at him and then turn back to my sister.

Saskia's eyes roll upward. "I need a man not a puppy dog," she sighs. Carly, sitting next to her, snorts.

Whatever. I can't keep up with what she wants. First it was Jude, then Vice. Next, she'll be fucking Finn, God forbid. Though, I fucking hope not. At least Vice doted on her. I wasn't too happy when they first started sneaking around behind my back, but even I have to admit, he was good for her. He put up with her bullshit. The dickhead was probably even in love with her. Unlike that bastard Jude who broke her heart.

I drag my plate closer to continue eating what's left of my lunch. Saskia should make things up with Dino. I'm not about to remind my sister of what will happen if she doesn't, not in front of her friends.

Joseph will make a match for her. And it won't be one she'll like.

I look across the cafeteria as Vice makes a joke, making the new girl smile.

"Urgh, get a fucking room," I hear Saskia say.

In response, I shake my head. My neck feels stiff, and my hands are itching to fucking hit something.

Where do I know the new girl from? Who does she remind me of?

She's a dead ringer for Aurora, even her hair and eye color are the same. But Aurora was a mouse—timid as fuck. No. This girl is a wolf. The way she stares at me when she thinks I'm not looking, pouting her bow lips that would look perfect around my cock. There's a challenge in her pretty blue eyes. I want to own her, control her, and force her to do nasty things knowing she'd fucking enjoy them. And I'm as hard as anything just thinking about it.

Lunch ends and my eyes seek her out as she leaves with him.

Fucking Dino. I hope he knows what the hell he's getting into because she's got the same fucked-up vibe as my sister, only shades darker.

What the hell is she doing with fucking Vice?

He can't help himself. Inexplicably drawn to the psychos.

Just like me.

All through classes, I couldn't fucking concentrate. I kept seeing her out of the corner of my eye. I don't know if it's Aurora haunting me, or the new girl. It's probably both. Even now, I can't stop watching her.

If I'm not careful I'm going to turn into a fucking stalker.

And we all know what happens after that…

SEVEN

VIOLA

OVER THE NEXT few days at Sacred Heart, I do all the things a student is supposed to—go to class, study in the library, attend hockey practice. I even meet with the slimy headmaster and do my best not to shove my pencil in his eye when his gaze wanders.

I also do all the things a good stalker does too.

I work out Lorcan's routine. I sit a few rows behind him in assembly. I know what time he gets into school. What time he usually leaves. What classes he has. What he eats. Who his friends are. I also know when he takes a dump and which bathroom he prefers.

But stalking is the easy part.

The issue isn't not knowing my target. It's getting him alone that's going to be difficult. His raucous friends follow him every-where like a toxic shadow. His sister is the worst. Wherever Duke or his friends are, she's never far behind.

I messaged Quinn at the beginning of the week asking her to dig out every last piece of information she could on the five top crime families whose sons and daughters attend Sacred Heart. I need to know *everything* there is to know about them if I'm to get Duke alone.

I don't have to wait long. By Thursday afternoon during class, there's a reply from Quinn and a new folder in the vault. It's huge and filled with files on Duke and on each one of his entourage. Quinn is nothing but thorough.

While the teacher drones in the background, I open the folder on my phone, noting the filenames of the reports inside:

1. *Duke (Saskia Evelyn, Lorcan James)*
2. *Baron (Finlay)*
3. *Earlshore (Carlotta)*
4. *Vice (Kristian, Kardinal)*
5. *Marques (Jude Luther, Cecilia Grace, ~~Aurora May~~,*
   ~~Byron Saint~~)

I take a few minutes to swipe through each report. There are hundreds of news articles, medical records, therapist notes, and even financial data on some of the names in the list. It's going to take some time to read through it all.

There's a lot of information on Finlay Baron and his messed-up family. I skip him, mostly because he doesn't appeal to me in the slightest.

The Vice brothers I take my time over. Interesting to note, Vice has an older brother. Kristian—an older, more serious looking Dino from his picture. He doesn't attend Sacred Heart now, but he used to. I'm glad Quinn has included him in the report because it might help me work out Vice's weakness. Although, I have an inkling as to what that is already.

The Marques and the Earlshores have less coverage, clearly they're not as scandalous. I have no interest in Carly, but the client's daughter, Cecilia Marques, Aurora's older sister, is someone I should speak to.

Jude Luther Marques also goes to this school, but he's Cecilia's cousin on her father's side. The picture of him shows a golden-haired jock in a rugby shirt, and a smolder to his dark brows. I note that he was Sacred Heart's rugby captain and best fly-half in years until he was suspended for drinking. Quinn must have added him to the list because he's a Marques and therefore one of *The Five*, but I've yet to meet him.

I skip and move on to the last file, and I'm surprised to see how short it is. Mostly it's about their father. Lorcan and Saskia themselves are hardly mentioned in their scant report, but there's a note from Quinn on that. Someone went to great lengths to remove or hide all mentions of them from all databases, public or otherwise.

If I want to get to know my prey, I'm going to have to do it the old-fashioned way—gossiping with my classmates.

The bell rings. Everyone around me starts packing up their things, heading off to their next class. I haven't seen Duke since lunchtime so I'm sure he won't be in double French. A plain-looking girl with long brown hair and glasses nearest to me looks like an easy target so I give her a winning smile.

"One of the girls, Carly I think her name was, mentioned a boathouse? Do you know where it is?"

"Through the quad and out the rear of the building. Take the pathway through the fields to get to the lake. But don't go alone. Make sure you take a buddy with you. The school doesn't want anyone walking anywhere on campus alone after what happened to that girl." She slips her bag onto her shoulder, eyes narrowing. "You're new aren't you?"

"Word gets around, huh?" I say as we both walk out of class and into the hall.

She stops outside of the classroom. "No. I read about you. Victoria, right? We don't get many transfer students here, given the godawful reputation of the patrons," she says, eyes flitting upward.

She holds out her hand. I don't take it, and it doesn't seem to bother her. "I'm Laura. If you need anything, refuge from the sharks, you can find me in there." She points across the hall to the library.

"Sharks?" I repeat.

"Oh that's just what they say." She scoffs. "That this is a school just full of sharks all looking for their next meal."

"And Saskia Duke is *the* Great White?"

She laughs. "Something like that."

The boathouse consists of two parts—a storage side filled with boats, and a communal lounge area with bi-folding doors that open out onto the dock. A lone car is parked in the driveway. I recognize the Bugatti as Lorcan's, but there are no lights on inside the building, and when I knock no one answers. Once I'm convinced the place is empty, I sneak inside.

Even in the depths of winter, the place still smells like summer. It's full of expensive but comfortable chairs and sofas. Playing cards, empty bottles of whiskey and vodka, and casino chips spread over the middle of the glass coffee table. Artwork hangs on the soft-hued blue walls. There's even a portable speaker set up on a side unit.

I slip a few bugs under the lampshades and behind the art, and then leave it like I was never there.

As I'm walking back, the perfect moment to follow Duke arises. Looking the immaculate student I know he's not, he's talking on his phone as he traipses through the school gardens toward the boathouse, possibly to collect his car. My pulse quickens. I follow behind far enough that he shouldn't see me even if he turned around.

As soon as he enters the boathouse, I switch on the listening device installed as an app on my phone that connects to the bugs I just dropped inside, and hunker down behind a tree to listen. It's a one-sided conversation.

"We've got what you want. Delivery on Friday as planned."

"No, tonight is too short notice."

"No. No. I told you. She's not fucking part of it."

Silence.

And then...

"What part of *she's not fucking part of it* do you not understand? That wasn't the fucking deal."

There's a loud bang as he throws something, and it breaks. "Fucker," he says out loud. Then there's the sound of him walking over to the other side of the room before he calls someone else.

"We're not doing this anymore. They can go fucking screw themselves." He hangs up, slams the door, and drives off in his over-priced car.

Like any good spy, I hurry back though the communal gardens to the main parking lot behind the building to retrieve my car. I drive as fast as I can out of the school grounds, down the winding lanes, and away from the school.

The thrill of chasing my prey whips through me, making my toes tingle and my fingers itch. Flying around dark corners in a fast car, as the light seeps from the world, has my heart racing.

This is what I live for.

This fucking moment right here.

I get to the main road.

No Bugatti.

Shit. I should have slipped a tracker on his car while I had the chance. I hate it when I miss the obvious or make easy mistakes. It means I'm not focused. And I should be.

This is how you lose, Viola. And you can't fucking lose to anyone.

I drive some more. It takes me several minutes to get to the village surrounding the school. After some fruitless driving through it, I pull over and hit the steering wheel until the pent-up energy boiling through my veins subsides and I'm feeling less irate with myself. Only one thing gets me this pissed off—*Losing.*

Okay, where would he go? Home?

I call Quinn.

"His address wasn't in the intel I was given," I say as soon as she answers.

"Hold on, I'm sending it through now," she says, catching her breath.

"Did I call you in the middle of a workout?"

"I'm running." She breathes sexily down the line. "You should try it sometime."

"I'm always running," I say flippantly.

I hang up and check the secure folder Quinn uses to share files. Inside is a new note containing an address. *111 Rosebury Drive.* I check the map. It's not too far from here. If I'd have widened my search, I'd have found him.

Two minutes later, I'm parked close enough to his house that I can see his glistening black Bugatti parked in a perfect position on the drive. I'm far enough away from his house that if anyone looks out the window, they wouldn't be able to see me.

The prickle of excitement is back, like a familiar friend caressing my edges. It's times like this I don't even think I'm inside my body, no longer tethered to this earth. I'm high up, looking way down.

I drag in a slow breath. *Time to focus.*

Because it's a long way to fall if I fuck this up.

I don't have to wait long. Duke comes out of the house looking severely pissed. He gets back in his car and pulls off the driveway through the huge gates. I wait a few, and then tail him.

About a mile or so out of the village we get to the entrance of another private school—The Norton Priory School for Girls, I note from the black and green billboard outside. Not a place I would expect Duke to visit.

The Bugatti idles outside until a blonde girl in a blue and green check uniform comes out of it. She sees Duke's car, annoyance flashing over her pretty snub face. I snap a few pictures of her as she walks over to where his car is waiting and climbs inside.

If this is a hook up, it's a boring one. It looks like they're just talking. Minutes later, she's exiting the car and going back into the school. Duke doesn't drive off though. He's still there, waiting.

What are you playing at, Lorcan? Who is that girl? Your next victim?

I share the pictures I took of the blonde girl with Quinn. *If anyone can find out who she is...*

Suddenly, Duke gets out of his car and heads in my direction. I'm parked slightly around a bend, quite a way back. *How did he see me? Has he seen me or is he just going for a walk?*

He keeps on approaching, eyes trained on my Mercedes.

Fuck. He's seen me.

I have seconds to decide if I want to drive off or stay my ground. I can't blow my cover, and I have no excuse for being here. *Fucking hell.* I jam my foot on the pedal and reverse spin, turning the car around to zoom off.

In my rear-view mirror, Duke, standing stock-still, frown marring his beautiful features, watches me speed away.

He's clocked the plate.

Great.

Now I need to get rid of this fucking car.

EIGHT

VIOLA

FRIDAY MORNING, I meet Dante at a service station to trade cars. I open the driver side door of the Merc, tossing the keys to him as I step outside, rubbing my arms since there's a balmy autumn breeze this morning. I'm in my school uniform already, minus the blazer, about to head in.

Dante's eyes seem to bug out of his head for a brief second as he looks at me. His gaze zips down to my bare legs beneath my short, pleated skirt, and then back up to where they should be. He looks pained, as though the very sight of me burns his retinas.

"Can you cover up?"

"What the fuck are you talking about? This is what I have to wear to that shitty school."

"You dress like that? The skirt's all the way up your ass."

I grit my teeth, mostly to prevent them chattering rather than because I'm annoyed. "And?" This guy has seen me in cut out PVC and skin-tight latex, with all sorts of body parts on display. Not once has he reacted like this.

I cross my arms, hugging myself over the thin shirtsleeves.

It's kind of endearing.

He throws his jacket at me.

I sigh but slip it on, enjoying the warmth from when he was wearing it. I look around the empty lot.

How did he get here?

"Where's the replacement?"

"It was too short notice," he sighs.

"How quickly can you get me a new one?" I ask him.

"Do I look like your local garage?" he says, opening the door to the Merc to get in, sliding his long legs behind the wheel.

I lean against the door frame as he adjusts the seat to fit his taller, imposing self. "Stop being a prick. I need a car."

His icy blue eyes regard me stoically. "You have one. What happened to the Beetle?"

He means my *actual* car. The car bought in Viola's name, currently parked on Viola's driveway. Dante has seen my sage green VW Beetle a total of three times, and all of those times I had switched the plates to prevent him from finding out where the damn thing is registered.

I do not need him to know where I live. It's not personal. It's just good business. Apart from the cabin, I know nothing about him. We might wake up one day with each other as a target, so why make it easier?

I draw my lips into a straight line. "*Victoria*, the schoolgirl, needs a car. You know she can't drive the Beetle."

He exhales. "When?"

"Tomorrow."

"I'll try and get you something, but I can't guarantee it *that* soon," he says, the muscle in his jaw ticking over. "Have you figured out the job yet? It's been a week, V."

He wants to know if I've decided when and how I'm going to do it. Jobs usually take a few hours to a few days max. I should have a location in mind at least by now...

I don't.

Why the fuck is Dante probing? He's not my mentor anymore, and we're not on this job together.

Ignoring the question, I go back to the original issue. "What am I supposed to do then? I need a car."

"So you've said. I don't know, get a taxi. Didn't you hire a Bentley?"

Polina would crucify me if I expense too much of that shit. I shrug at him. "You know how it goes."

He sighs, turning the engine over. "With those legs on display, you could always hitchhike your way in."

By the time a taxi arrives, I'm already late for damn school. I barge into my first class twenty minutes after the bell has rung. Every student in the room looks up. I slip into the only empty seat in the room near the front.

Duke is with the rest of his posse at the back of the classroom. He doesn't seem to notice when I enter or acknowledge me throughout the class, leading me to think I was wrong yesterday. *Maybe he didn't see me.*

The day goes slowly. Too slowly. Somehow, I've lost Duke's attention. To gain it back, I need to get right in his face.

"Let's sit with your friends today," I say to Vice as we approach the cafeteria. He's been waiting for me at my locker every day to walk with me to lunch, and it's stopping me from doing my actual fucking job. But I can't alienate Vice just yet. He might be useful.

He frowns at me, his blue eyes sparkling like twin sapphires. "You want to sit with the Dukes?"

I shrug. "Why not. You keep saying you want to piss Saskia off. What better way than to rub it in her face."

He gives me an evil grin. "You're not as sweet as you look, are you? Oh, hold on." He slips his phone out of his pocket and looks at it, a dark look shadowing his pretty face. "Head in without me. I need to take this."

He answers it as he walks away. "This had better be good. I'm fucking busy." Is all I hear before he moves out of earshot.

Inside the cafeteria, I make a beeline for the table most favored by Lorcan's inner circle. The Dukes, Baron and Earlshore are already seated. Lorcan is in the center talking over the finer points of team sports with the dirty blonde sitting next to him—Finlay Baron. One of Lorcan's closest buddies, and who I now know is the only son of the infamous retired arms dealer, Midas Baron.

Saskia, deep in thought, scrolling through her phone, gives me the barest glance. It's Carly next to her who speaks up. "This is a private table."

I place my tray down. "Is there such a thing in a school cafeteria?" I say. I'm pretty sure I can sit where I like.

Finn stops talking and gives me a once over that makes my skin crawl. I already know his type. "Oh, it's the tasty new girl. Has Vice let you out of his sight?"

I give him a blank look. "I'm here to eat lunch."

He shakes his head. "You can't sit there… unless you want to nominate yourself for the vote." There's a creepy light in his eyes all of a sudden.

"What vote?"

"He means the vote to be one of our whores," says Lorcan without a flicker of emotion.

If looks could fuck you blind and leave you gasping for more, his would. A tight, coil of desire snakes through my entire body without reason, or my permission, bringing the darkness with it.

I tighten my fingers on my tray.

It's the only outward indication of my reaction to him.

I focus on his words. Or one word in particular—*whores*. I've seen girls coming over to Lorcan's table ever since I got here, only to be turned away by Finn or one of the other guys. I assumed those girls were trying to get Lorcan's attention.

Now, it seems I'm one of those girls.

But they don't have the agenda I do.

My brain, as usual, has other thoughts now my body is triggered. *Is that what it takes to get him alone? Do I have to fuck him? Is that what he's implying?*

74

I need to know more.

I cock my head at him. "Explain."

He rakes his eyes over me, as though it's just the two of us in the room alone. "You'd belong to us in every way possible. And I mean every fucking way."

"Us?" But I already know.

Lorcan gestures to the table. "Me, Shitboy here. Oh, and Vice of course. Marques too, though you haven't met yet. Some girls enjoy having four cocks at once." His features remain deadpan, but the challenge is there, in his eyes if you look hard enough. If he wanted to shock me, it's not going to work.

I don't do shock. My body can feel things and go places, but it's like I'm a casual observer until the darkness sweeps me up inside a cocoon of rage. And then, I can't control it.

I mull over his offer. In contrast to my hobbies, I don't like to fuck just anyone, four-way aside. Disgust comes just as easily as lust. But if I have to use my body like that, I can. I just won't take part.

Something tells me though, that this one likes to chase way too much.

And I can be the *perfect* mouse.

I cock my head to the side. "Why would I do that?"

"The benefits, tasty new girl," Finn chimes in. "You get to be part of *our* exclusive circle."

"Why do they call you Shitboy?" I can't help but ask.

"Because I prefer to fuck bitches up the ass," shrugs Finn.

"Urgh, fucking gross, Finn. Do you have to be such a pervert?" Carly exclaims.

"What? She asked, so I'm telling her."

Saskia huffs out a long-winded sigh. "If she wants to nominate herself, fine, but she's not sitting with us. Whores aren't welcome here."

Lorcan flicks his gaze to his sister. "I decide who sits with us." He looks back at me. "So what's it to be, Victoria?"

Behind Lorcan, Vice has entered the cafeteria, heading toward us.

"Thanks, but I'll pass." Playing their games might get me closer to my target, but the moment I let these assholes here call the shots, Duke will lose the hard-on he has for me. I want to keep him longing and desperate.

Because… that's how I win.

"Thought so," Lorcan snorts, nostrils flaring. "Fuck off then."

His reaction makes me smile inside.

"What a fucking mess," Dino mutters as he saunters up, shoving his cell into his pocket. He shoots a look at Saskia, and then everyone else staring at me. "Oh. She's with me."

"You've got a nerve. Who the fuck gave you permission to sit with us?" Lorcan drawls.

"Your sister did," says Vice, pulling out his chair, sliding into it. He gestures for me to do the same. I lower myself into the empty chair beside him.

Saskia glowers at us both but doesn't contradict her ex.

"Fuck it, fine. Have at it," Lorcan snaps.

Carly glances at her friend and then cocks her head at Dino. "You're such a wanker."

"Ah, so you did miss me during my extended leave." He grins at her.

"It's called suspension. And fuck no. Although, I'll admit you're easier on the eyes than Finn."

"Hey, what the fuck?" Finn gives a hurt look.

"You're coming next Saturday, right?" Carly continues.

Dino nods, stealing a fry off my plate and eating it.

"Are you bringing her?" Lorcan suddenly asks.

Her? I'm sitting right here, dickhead.

"To the party? I'll be there. Tory won't." Vice answers.

If this is Duke's exclusive, invite-only party that happens once a month, I can't miss that.

"Why not? I'm free Saturday," I say looking at Vice.

"It's not the type of party you're used to," Vice says, flashing some unspoken warning at me. This only makes me want to go even more. And what does he know what I'm used to? He knows fuck all about me, and only what I want him to know.

"Has this got something to do with the vote?"

Lorcan lounges in his chair, not taking his eyes off me. "No, the vote happens a few days before."

"Then, I'm in," I say nonchalantly.

My would-be-protector frowns, red hair hanging over his eyes. He runs a hand through it, smoothing it back. "Are you sure?"

"I said I'm in."

Lorcan smirks, chartreuse-green eyes practically glowing. "You heard her, she's in."

"She can't come to the party and not be part of the vote," says Finn, adding his two-fucking-cents in one of those nasal voices you can't really stand. If I cared enough to damage his voice box so that he couldn't ever speak again, I would.

Lorcan looks straight at me. "Actually, Shitboy's right."

Finn gives a slow smile.

"She's not fucking part of it, alright," Vice says. He glances at me. "We're dating."

I shoot him a look, brows raised. *News to me.*

Carly sucks in a breath. Finn chuckles, clearly loving this. Lorcan looks annoyed.

Under the table, Vice squeezes my leg almost making me jump out of my seat. I smother the urge to elbow him in the gut, and concentrate on returning a fixed-look to the other side of the table. I do, however, wrap Vice's hand in mine and grip hard.

My nails alone will draw blood.

Vice stiffens but he doesn't jerk away. I'm not looking at his face, so I don't know how he's taking my little declaration of love.

"I held back the other day, Vice, because you're like a brother to me. But you keep on fucking disrespecting my sister," Lorcan says, in a dangerously low tone of voice.

Saskia, eyes bulging out of her head, scrapes her chair back and stands up. "Oh, just fucking stop it, Lor. All of you. You're all

77

a bunch of fuckwits. If he wants this piece of trash whore to be his girlfriend and bring her to the stupid party, let him. I dumped him, remember."

Lorcan's jaw clenches, but the anger drains away quickly leaving him blank-faced and closed off. "Fine, Sas. If you're okay with it, I don't have a problem."

Saskia tosses her hair. "Good." She storms off with Carly following not far behind.

"You sure know how to stir the pot." Finn chuckles at Vice.

"Bring her Saturday, and don't be late," Lorcan says. He gives me one last look and then turns away.

"Girlfriend?" I say to Vice after everyone's interest has waned, prying his hand off my leg. I'm pleased to see angry red crescent marks all over it

He grimaces. "Sorry about that. You don't want to go there single. That's not a game you want to play. Lorcan's parties can get a little fucked-up."

"You'll be there to protect me?" I mean it sarcastically, but he melts before my eyes.

"Of course, baby. Stick with me. I'll look after you." His blue eyes are filled with lust, but as he glances over to where Saskia Duke is leaving the cafeteria anyone can see the heart-breaking despair he's trying to hide still lurking in their depths.

NINE

VIOLA

I'M SO CAUGHT up in stalking Duke in the first week that I forget all about updating Polina. I awake to the shrill sound of my phone in the middle of the night.

Cursing and squinting in the dark, I reach for it on the side table. As soon as I switch on the side table light, I sit up and connect the call. "Why are you calling me at 4 a.m.?"

"The client called me. His other daughter is missing," Polina hisses down the phone.

"What?" I blink myself awake.

"Where's the target?"

"He went home last night." The sigh leaves my lips before I can stop it. Obviously, I didn't follow him home or sit outside all night to make sure of it. I even had to take a cab to the apartment since I don't have a car except the Beetle right now.

"I need you to track his daughter down and bring her home."

"Finding lost kids isn't really my job."

"I don't give a fuck. The client is going fucking nuts."

That's so far beyond the scope of what I do. "I'm not a fucking babysitter, Polina. Use one of your other guys."

81

"This is what you've been paid for. This is not a request. Find her or I'll replace you."

"And what if she recognizes me from school?" I've not met Cecilia yet but my picture has been all over the school online newspaper.

"Your problem to solve."

She hangs up before I can respond.

With Quinn's help, I track Cecilia Marques to a shitty warehouse rave in the middle of an industrial site just as the sun starts its ascent in the morning sky. This place isn't legal. It has a barricaded, chained-up doorway that you have to squeeze through just to get inside. I can hear the thud of music from up here as I clamber into the dilapidated warehouse.

Trash lines the piss-ridden stairwell. A couple of junkies going at it in the entryway ignore me as I open the door of the bar with a heavy shove. In the inner sanctum, the place is rowdy, pulsing with music. All I can see is a sea of bodies, smoke, and strobe lighting.

What a way to start the weekend.

I hate these places, being no good with physical contact of any kind. Still, if I need to enter this room and allow all of these drunk, sweaty people to touch me, for the sake of a job, fine. *But I can't promise anything.*

About halfway in, I spot Cecilia standing at the bar. I know it's her because I've seen her a few times in school this week. I hesitate when I see Duke with her, his arm casually draped around her shoulder. *What the fuck is he doing here with my client's daughter?*

The arrogant asshole takes a large swig of his drink while staring out at the crowds.

He looks nothing like his picture now. Tattoos for days up both arms, faded undercut, lip pierced, torn black jeans, and a V neck shirt—vastly different to his more polished look at school.

Cecilia on the other hand looks nervous but determined in a

mini skirt and matching strapless corset as she stares out into the crowd, sipping a glass of clear liquid.

Duke says something to Cecilia and removes his arm away from her shoulder to type something on his phone. Then he downs the rest of his beer by knocking it back, slamming the empty on the bar. He rudely gestures to the bar staff to bring him another.

Fucking rich boys.

I watch for a few more minutes. They're both drinking a hell of a lot and scanning the crowd. It's as though they're both waiting for someone.

Hopefully, he's intoxicated enough that I could go over there and drag her ass home, and he wouldn't remember a thing the next day. I don't look like my uniformed self in a black leather skirt and a black cut-out midriff top. Silver loops to match my silver cross around my neck and silver skull, knuckle rings on all fingers of my left hand. My blond hair no longer covered by the hideous wig sweeps down past my shoulders.

I'm good at blending in.

Still, I should probably approach with caution, like you would a stray, savage dog.

Suddenly, he perks up and nudges Cecilia. She bites her lip and gathers herself. The look on her face is one I've seen many times before but never understood—hopeless resignation. A girl with several piercings, pink hair, and denim hot pants appears. She indicates to Cecilia and Duke to go with her, and they disappear into the crowd.

I follow at a distance. Over the throbbing music and flashing lights, I can barely make out their heads as they cut through the crowd, making a beeline for the corner of the club. I'm just in time to see them enter a doorway marked private.

I push through the sweaty bodies, gagging with revulsion at the feel of their slick bodies sliding over mine. I get to the door. It's not locked so I slowly push it open. Inside is a long, empty corridor filled with pink neon floor lights and lined with doors.

Moans and screams come from behind each one as I pass by. I peer into one and see a couple going at it in a sex swing. Another room has three men spit roasting a girl strapped naked to a bench.

This is not the type of place I ever imagined two kids from an elite prep school would enjoy. Still, to each their own.

The fifth door down has a guy stripped down to his boxer shorts, chained up by his arms and legs. He's wearing a black hood so he's completely sensory deprived. The sight of him makes me stop and stare. Those swirling tattoos up both arms cover his torso completely—I recognize them. Lorcan has some crazy ink littered with masonic symbols that reek of his fucking family coat of arms on one of his forearms.

You've got to be fucking kidding me.

Of all the luck. It's Duke tied up in a pretty bow, just for me.

Blood rushes to my head as I step into the room and close the door behind me. He jerks his head toward the sound, but hooded the way he is, he can't see me. It would be so fucking easy to slice him from throat to groin.

So easy.

But these kinds of places, even illegal ones, have cameras.

Sure enough, there are two in each opposite far corner.

Underneath my skirt is the five-inch dagger I carry with me everywhere. I palm it now and stalk my prey by walking around him in a slow circle, every so often knocking the edge of the blade on the top of my thigh-high boot. He cocks his head, listening intently.

I had no idea Lorcan was into this kind of thing.

Then again, it doesn't surprise me, given his penchant for raping and murdering little girls. Maybe he likes to feel what his victims go through. Because Aurora isn't his first. I can promise you that.

He tries to speak but his voice comes out muffled. It sounded like he asked, 'who the fuck are you?' but I can't be sure.

He must be gagged under there.

I wet my lips, letting the smile that wants to play across my lips come out for the first time since I took this fucking job.

"Your worst nightmare," I say softly, taking the point of my knife and running it down his taut body, making him quiver in anticipation. For a senior, his body is beautifully sculpted. I take advantage of that and draw my blade over each muscle, nicking a vein here and there, enticing blood to the surface. He hisses with every cut but doesn't tell me to stop.

It agonizes me that I can't just end him now. One quick swipe, that's all it would take. I'd even remove his hood so my eyes would be the last thing he saw. If I wasn't being paid to make it look like an accident, I wouldn't fucking hesitate.

I want him to know I was doing this for Aurora.

For Cecilia.

Fuck.

My job.

I still need to do that.

"Where's Cecilia?" I ask him.

He doesn't reply so I drag the sharp edge of my dagger down the side of his neck ever so lightly, making him stay absolutely still, over his collarbone and down his chest. My dagger is razor-edged so blood spills to the surface.

A sound outside draws me back to reality. She must be in one of these rooms.

"Aurora sends her love," I whisper at him. With a kiss on his lips through the hood, I leave the room.

The next room has Cecilia in it, chained up by her wrists hanging in the center of the room. Unlike Lorcan, she's completely naked, not a strip of clothing on her except for a ball gag in her mouth.

She's also not alone. There's a guy with his pants down behind her. The guy hasn't heard me come in. Cecilia has though. Her tear-stained eyes dart to me, pleading for help.

I don't even have to think twice.

Fuck the cameras.

I put my fingers to my lips, telling her to be quiet, and walk up behind the sicko about to rape her. Grabbing the back of his head, I cleanly and evenly slit his throat. He gurgles and collapses—a hot mess of blood coating us both.

It's only then that I recognize him.

It's the paedo-teacher from the common room.

Cecilia is a blubbering mess as she watches me sheath my knife. She doesn't fucking stop when I start undoing the chains digging into her wrists and remove the gag.

"We need to leave," I say firmly, as she falls into my arms.

She nods, sobs wrack her bruised body.

I'm almost tempted to leave her here, she's being so pathetic. But she's seen my face. Yes, there are cameras but I'm hoping they're for show. If they're not, I'll have to ask Quinn to see if she can wipe them remotely.

Looking around, I find a man's coat, so I throw it over her shoulders and bundle the rest of her clothes into her arms. "Put this on and wrap it around you. You need to act natural."

She nods again, stifling tears.

I'm tempted to go next door and finish the job on Duke completely, but something doesn't add up. *Why the fuck is Lorcan trussed up like a turkey for thanksgiving? And why is a teacher from Sacred Heart here, of all the fucked-up places.*

I'm aware this is not a time to procrastinate. Someone is going to find this body soon, and we need to be gone way before then.

I also don't like to kill unplanned.

This whole night is one complete impromptu fuckup.

I manage to steer a subdued Cecilia through the rave of bodies and then out to my car. Once she's in the passenger side, I engage the child lock and shut her in. I make my way to the driver's side.

She stares at me, cradling her clothes on her lap, eyes dropping to the knife strapped to my thigh as my skirt rides up.

I start the engine, shooting her a look. "Would you rather I left you to get raped?"

She hurriedly shakes her head.

When we get outside her family mansion at a glorious 8a.m.

on a Saturday morning, I give her an expectant look.

"Maybe you should sleep the day off? You look like shit."

Her brow creases but I don't care. I'm tired. Wearing a mask all day and all night is fucking tiresome. And dealing with teenagers on top of that? *Even worse.*

As she opens the door, she sees the cars in the drive and stops.

"Shitfuck. Jude's here," she says.

"Is he a problem?"

"No, no. Just an overprotective cousin. I wasn't expecting him, that's all."

Not a minute later, a tall, broad-shouldered guy with dark blonde hair and a brooding look on his face comes to the door. He stares at us, namely me, from the front steps. Quinn's files mentioned a Jude Marques. I make a mental note to read up on his connection to all of this. It doesn't look like the Marques family are the innocent victims at all.

Cecilia hesitates for a second, but then gets out and starts walking toward the house. Something out of place catches my eye. Her purse is still in the car, next to the seat.

"You forgot something," I call to her. I lean over to lift it out of the footwell and hand it to her as she comes back. I make the mistake of glancing at the towering blonde again. As soon as our eyes meet, a shiver runs through me that I suppress and ignore. He's pretty, and after my little knife party with Lorcan, my body is primed. But he's also a student, and Cecilia's cousin.

Definitely off limits.

"What about Lorcan?" Cecilia asks, taking the purse, snapping me out of my thoughts. She sounds more concerned than afraid. *Stockholm syndrome much?*

"Don't worry, I'll deal with him," I say, offhandedly.

She nods, grimacing as though in pain as she straightens. "He pretends he can take it, but they're going to kill him one day."

I don't know what she means by that, but I store it away. I drive off back to my place thinking…

Oh, *fucking so am I.*

TEN

JUDE

CECE, eyes stained panda black with make-up, gives me a wary look as she sidesteps me in the hall. I grab her by the arm as she tries to slip by me.

"Who was that?" I jut my chin at the car reversing out of the driveway on the security monitors. All I caught was a cascade of white-blonde hair as the bitch drove away.

"Let go of me, Jude. You're drunk," Cece says, voice firm though her lips are quivering. In fact, her whole body is shaking.

"Whose coat are you wearing? Is that a man's coat?" I'm livid. Livid with the guys for getting her involved in this crap, livid with the girls for ducking out. We have a system. You do not fuck with the system.

"It's no one's. Now let me go. You're hurting me."

Her words are like daggers in my chest. I release her and stand there like a douche as she massages her arm where I held her too tight. Her wrists though, they look bruised. I wasn't holding her that hard.

"Jesus, I didn't do that, did I?" I take a step toward my cousin,

89

but she shuffles back like she's afraid. I hesitate and then stop moving. "Who hurt you?"

She flicks her eyes up to me, an accusatory glance cutting into me like glass. She shakes her head. "I need to go shower." Then, she's gone, disappearing into the vast, dimly lit house like she was never there.

Fuck. I'm losing her.

Just like Aurora.

Her purse is on the counter, so I take it and rifle through until I find her phone. It's unlocked so I swipe through quickly to see the last number dialed.

Lorcan.

Fucking bastard. I knew it. As if Aurora wasn't enough. He has to go and drag Cecilia into his fucking bullshit games. He took her somewhere last night, and it wasn't for some cozy fucking date either.

I press dial and wait for the fucker to answer his phone. It just goes straight to voicemail. Wherever he is, he's underground or doesn't have signal. Not that he'll tell me jack shit. Lor's a secretive little prick. He has been since eighth grade when he used to take all the girls I liked to the orchard first, and wouldn't tell me about it until after they chose him over me.

Cece isn't going to tell me fuck all either. And all that leaves is the bitch who dropped Cece off. She must know what happened.

I head to the downstairs office and open up the monitor where I can replay the feed from the security cameras. I scroll through the footage until I come to the part where Cece goes back to the car. The girl behind the wheel leans over just enough that you can see her face.

She's hot. White-blonde hair, almond shaped eyes. Just my type. I take a snap of the car, a black VW, with my phone and sent it to a guy I know who has tabs on all the CCTV footage for miles around.

I don't know who she is, but I'm going to find the fuck out. And make her tell me everything.

And then I'm going to bury that sly fucker Lorcan six feet under for what he did to Cece, and Aurora, and then I'll dance on his shitting grave.

ELEVEN

VIOLA

MY FIRST RUN in with the infamous Jude Marques is in the hallway on Monday morning.

I'm wearing my Aurora wig. My blue contacts are in and my face is clean of makeup, but he must know who I am because he storms over like the devil incarnate.

The ex-golden boy of Sacred Heart slams the door of my locker door, making it rattle. Students around us are staring. Fuck, I'm staring. *What the hell is he playing at?* Not letting my annoyance show, I angle my head up at him, looking bored. He looks like he was dragged through a hedge backwards, and then thrown off a cliff for good measure. He also reeks of booze. I get it. He doesn't fucking care. Out of everything, that's what I like about him. His file was detailed enough for me to know he's otherwise pretty reckless, and absolutely fucking stupid. Fighting, stealing, vandalism, even arson. Everything he does expends energy. If there was a person who was the complete opposite of me—it would be Jude Marques.

"You need to leave," he spits at me.

"Excuse me?"

He moves away from the locker and comes in close. "I know why you're here. Cecilia doesn't need you or want you, so you can fucking leave."

"I'm here for the same reason you are. I'm here to learn."

Jude's eyes blaze. "I checked you out. Just transferred here only last week. Convenient that."

What the fuck, why is this asshole digging into what's none of his business?

"I don't know what you're talking about. I transferred because my mother relocated."

"Lying cunt," he snarls.

Okay, that's it.

"Get the fuck out of my way," I say, giving him the warning most men never get. "I don't have time for this."

I've faced many imposing men in my life. They're bigger, stronger, and obviously dumber. Jude does what all men think they have a right to do—he grabs me and hauls me into an empty classroom. He's not gentle or discreet. A number of students are outright gaping at us. My gut reaction is to smack his nose into his fucking skull, breaking it, but that would draw questions. I'm on the job, and we just happen to be in the one place I can't take liberties. *Even if he fucking touched me.*

He kicks the door closed, glares at the students trying to peer in, and then turns on me with insidious eyes. "How much is he paying you?"

I suck in a breath and give him a dark look. "How much is *who* paying me?"

"Lorcan." He snarls. "I know it was you who brought Cece home. She cracked in the end, told me where he took her."

I raise a brow. "I've no idea what you're talking about." Of course Cecilia was going to say something to Jude after I dropped her off. What did I expect?

"Don't play games. It was you. I tracked your car to the over-spill carpark. You look different now. Your hair…" He chokes. "What are you? A rat? Is he paying you to spy on me?"

So much for driving the Beetle to school. I thought I could get away with it so far away from the entrance.

I place my books on the desk next to me and straighten my uniform. "Okay. Just who is it you think I am?"

"I'm the one asking the questions here. Who are you? What is he paying you to do?" he sneers, eyes narrowing.

Cat's out of the bag now. I warned Polina this would happen. "To protect your cousin."

"Bullshit."

"Cece told you I saved her, right?"

Color returns to his face. "She said you stopped it from happening."

I purse my lips and say nothing.

"I don't know how," he snorts. "I mean look at you, you're fucking tiny. I could knock you out like that," he says with a click of his fingers.

I'd like to see you try, asshole.

With a sigh, I tug up the hem of my skirt showing him the edge of my blade strapped to my thigh.

The look on his face is worth it.

I roll my eyes. "Just move out my fucking way, and let me do my job."

"And what job is that, standing by while innocent girls get raped? Or spreading your legs? Because I think you're lying. You're one of his whores, aren't you?" He sneers.

"You're wrong," I say, picking my books up off the table. "Now…" I walk right up to Jude until I'm too close for him to move without me moving first. "If you'll excuse me. I have classes to get to. I may be fucking tiny, but I do know which artery bleeds out the fastest." I ruin the effect by having to look up at him, but he's so tall I'd have to wear a pair of nine-inch heels to just be on an even keel.

He glares at me, shaking his head. "You're not needed. She's not going anywhere with that fucker without me, so you can piss off."

"Are you sure about that? Did you stop it from happening last time?" I've no idea if there was even a last time, but he doesn't know that.

He breaks contact first, running a hand through his mussed-up hair. Let him believe what he wants to believe.

As his hazel eyes seek me out again, they flash with unmissable pain. "I wasn't there for Aurora. God knows..." His eyes narrow as he breathes, the space between us clouding with the heavy aroma of alcohol. "Fine. But you call me the minute he pulls another fucking stunt like last night."

"I'll get your number from Cece," I say sweetly, playing along. I'll let Jude think he's winning… for now.

Jude continues to give me a murderous stare, but after a pause shifts aside to let me pass.

I exit the classroom just as the bell rings.

What the fuck just happened?

I called it. I knew it would happen. Playing both sides was going to get my cover blown. Still, Jude has no clue who I really am, and I need it to stay that way if I'm going to get this job done without getting caught.

I just hope he doesn't talk to Lorcan, because then the shit will really hit the fan.

In the evening, I get a message from Polina that the client is not that happy with me, and that Quinn is working on wiping the footage of the sex club. Polina already called me less than a day ago to rag me out for not finishing the job at the nightclub. She has a point. I still don't know why I hesitated myself.

Maybe I want to play with Duke some more. Maybe I want more of a challenge.

Who fucking knows?

"Jude Marques knows about me," I tell Dante on the secure line we have after getting him up to speed on the job. I may not want Dante to take credit for the kill, but sometimes you need a good sounding board.

"So you weren't careful?"

"He thinks I'm spying on him," I say, ignoring his jab. It's his fault for not getting me a new car in time.

"Your job is to dispose of Duke, not play detective."

"This doesn't sit right, and you know it."

"V," Dante says. "You can't just follow orders, can you?"

"Not when the client is fucking lying, no I can't."

"It's simple wet work. Get shit done and get out. Or have I taught you fuck-all?"

"You taught me not to rush in and get fucked by the agency. Something feels off. You know my gut is always right."

He laughs down the phone.

"What's so funny?" I don't find this funny at all.

"You and your fucking intuition. You wanted this job, and I'm telling you not to question it. There are things you don't know about that I can't tell you. But if you screw this up, it will get ugly. And I can't help you if it does."

"I don't need your help. Never have. And where's the replacement car you promised me?"

"You'll have it soon."

"Soon isn't good enough," I say, before hanging up.

I spend the next day watching Duke like a hawk. They didn't kill him, whoever *they* are. Cecilia was worried about nothing. Duke was back in school Monday morning acting like nothing happened. Come late Tuesday afternoon, he's even acting the model student.

I'm sitting in the library watching him from across the room, and have been for hours. He's studying, which is unusual. By now, he's almost always at the boathouse.

I check my watch again. Fuck. I need to give Polina another

update soon. After the last week of avoiding her, she's now demanding daily updates after school. Tedious. At least I'm back on track. I have an idea of how and when I'm going to take him out. Maybe I could call her now since Duke is clearly not going anywhere.

I'm beginning to think I've got his routine wrong when Saskia, Cecilia, and Carly walk in.

Saskia, with the same intense green eyes as her brother, though hers seem to be permanently filled with scorn, darts to me and then back to Lorcan.

Cecilia also sees me, but I refuse to look at her. Instead, I keep my head down and adjust the earpiece connected to the bug I casually placed on the underside of Lorcan's table during my trip to the bathroom.

"Lor, there you are," Saskia says, with a voice that could cut marble as it crackles in my inner right ear. "Are you coming? We want to get to the boathouse before it gets dark."

Lorcan looks up, focusing on his sister. "I meant what I said earlier. I'm done with it all," he says, his tone dismissive.

"I don't think that's—" Cecilia starts.

"This isn't a discussion," Lorcan snaps, cutting her off.

Saskia glares at him. "What are you even doing here?"

"Studying. What else?" he sighs.

"Why the fuck are you doing that? Your grades are perfect."

When he doesn't answer she takes a seat opposite him, pulling books from her bag. Carly and Cecilia join her on the same side and do the same.

Lorcan suddenly stops writing. "What the fuck are you three doing?"

"What does it look like, we're studying here with you," says Saskia.

He looks at his sister blankly. "I didn't say you could."

"And I didn't ask your permission," she says, tossing her hair.

He breathes out an exasperated sigh. "Fuck it, fine. Do what you like."

A few minutes later, Jude walks in, a permanent swagger in

his step. My pulse speeds up a little as he sees me all the way down the other end of the library, a dark look crossing his face, then he rounds on the table where the Dukes are.

"Why are we in here?" He's keeping his voice low but not low enough I can't hear.

"Lor's out," I hear Saskia say.

I can't see Jude's face since he has his back to me, but I can hear the confusion in his voice. "What do you mean he's out?"

"I'm fucking done alright," Lorcan says in a level voice.

Jude shifts, leaning over the table. "There's no fucking walking away from this and you know it." His tone is pissed off. "If we don't do this, we're the ones who get fucked." He gives a harsh laugh, speaking louder. "Quite fucking literally."

"Jude. Keep your fucking voice down. We're not alone here," Saskia hisses. I imagine her flicking a glance at me.

"I couldn't give a fuck. After everything that's happened, there's no getting out," Jude snaps.

"Is that a threat, Marques?" Lorcan asks, not bothering to whisper.

"Not a threat. I just want to talk," Jude says in response.

"So talk."

"Not here. At the boathouse."

"I messaged Dino and Finn to meet us there," Saskia says, flipping her phone shut.

Lorcan closes the book he was trying to read and gathers his notes into his bag. He gets to his feet. When they all look at him, he glares at them, cocking his head. "So, are we fucking going or not?"

I wait for them to leave and then quickly pack up and follow them outside. Darkness has already set, but I can just make out the four of them heading to the parking lot. Seeing Jude with the Dukes has me on edge.

The ripe darkness within me is calling now that we're on the move, but I smother it in mundane tasks like making sure no one sees me.

I take a detour to the toilets and change from my uniform into a pair of black leggings, a black hoodie, and some taped up running shoes. Shoe designers like to add those reflective strips down the sides, the ones which could save your life. I like to think, though it would never happen, I'd be that person who needed reflective strips. The kind of person who goes running, who grows fucking basil, and watches movies with friends on the weekend.

Not the kind of person who straps a five-inch blade to their thigh and stalks four unsuspecting students to a boathouse in the middle of fucking nowhere.

The boathouse is lit up from within with mirror-bright windows and lanterns on the patio area outside that line the decking all the way to the lake. I'm crouched in the long grass, spying on the six of them with a pair of digital binoculars while the wind does all kinds of shit to my hair. I end up pulling my hood up, so it doesn't get in my way while watching the dramas going on inside.

Truth is, I'm no longer ready for action. The adrenaline has seeped away with the fucking cold, leaving me tired and irritable. I can even feel a headache coming on.

This had better be over fucking quickly.

Through my binoculars, Jude, slightly taller and broader, is getting up in Lorcan's face, shoving him backward.

"Is that all you've got, Marques? No wonder Aurora came to me. She knew you wouldn't have the fucking balls." Lorcan sneers, with a cruel twist to his mouth.

It's the wrong thing to say.

Jude lunges for Lorcan, wrapping his hands around his throat. Saskia screams, while Dino and Finn try to pry him off. Carly and Cecilia are just standing there watching the scene unfold. I don't blame them. It's entertaining, if nothing else. Any minute, Jude is going to kill Lorcan.

No you don't, you fucker. That's my job.

My instincts tell me that Jude, for all his bravado, doesn't have the balls, just like Lorcan said.

Lorcan on the other hand…

This is going to be interesting. Whatever is going on, the seven of them are obviously caught up in something to do with the club. Not that I should care. Doing my job should be my only concern.

As if reading my mind, my phone buzzes. I reach into my pocket and yank out my cell. On the screen is another message from Polina to call her.

She's chasing for an update again. I've never waited this long to make my move before. Then again, I've never had to enroll in a fucking school and deal with teenage brats before.

I quickly check back on Jude and Lorcan. Dino and Finn have finally peeled Jude off and he's posturing, knocking them off like flies since he's bigger than them both. Lorcan is staring at him like he's amused by the whole fucking thing. Saskia is fussing between the two, like she can't make her mind up which side to take. Carly is covering her mouth like she's trying not to bloody laugh. Cecilia is gone.

Fuck. Where the hell is the Marques girl?

My phone rings.

I need to answer that. Polina obviously couldn't wait. And since I'm in the middle of nowhere, now is as good a time as any. I take out my earpiece and answer.

"If I didn't know any better, I'd say you were avoiding me," she says immediately.

"We're not allowed phones in school."

"Is that meant to be a joke?" she hisses down the line.

"Not at all," I say, keeping my tone innocent and light. "I'm in the middle of doing my job right now. Can I update you later?"

"Do it soon, the client is breathing down my fucking neck."

"About that, I'm going to need access to Quinn some more."

She scowls. "You already have my top researcher in your bed, what else do you need?"

On that little nugget, she hangs up.

I'm pulled back to the entertainment by a car screeching out of the boathouse driveway. I just about recognize Jude's Aston Martin.

Slipping my earpiece back in, I catch the end of the conversation in the boathouse. The teens are talking amongst themselves about what to do about Jude. After a minute, they give up and leave—Saskia with Lorcan in his McLaren, Carly with Finn in his car, and Dino on his bike.

Cecilia must be with Jude.

Even if Lorcan was going off somewhere solo, I couldn't follow him if I wanted to. I still don't have a car, and if anything happened to him after their little lover's spat all fingers will be pointed at my client's own family.

No, tonight wouldn't have worked, which is why I'm counting on the party.

I just need to figure out what Jude is up to.

TWELVE

VIOLA

I DON'T SEE Lorcan in school all day Tuesday until I'm walking home.

Dante, for all his virtues, still hasn't provided me with a replacement car, and after Jude recognized it, I'm loath to use the Beetle. So I've decided to use it to my advantage. I've timed my walk home so that it coincides with Lorcan's usual exit from the school.

"Are you really fucking walking?" Lorcan asks as he drives up in his black Bugatti Veyron. It's worth five times that of my apartment, and then some.

"It's my driver's day off," I say coolly.

He gives me a deadpan look. "Get in. I'll take you."

"Fine," I say. Fast cars are a weakness of mine, and I really didn't want to walk.

He leans over and opens the door for me. The interior smells of leather and cherries. I slip into the bucket seat like it was made to hug my body. There's nothing inside the car that screams psychopathic killer, unless you count the extremely neat almost

Odd. It doesn't match the way the crime scene was left at all. The way Aurora was murdered suggests someone disorganized, uncontrolled. I can almost imagine Lorcan killing the way Dante does—fastidious in every facet of the scene and the crime itself. Or even the way I do—planning every last fucking detail.

If I was the killer, I'd pick my victims off when no one is looking, after school has ended, and take them far, far away so no one can tie the location to the killer. You don't shit on your own doorstep.

Like Lorcan's doing right now?

But true to his word, he's driving me toward home, or the house I've rented to look like a home, the right way after I gave him directions. Every so often Lorcan glances at me like he can't quite decipher me.

Apart from that, we drive in silence.

It's absolute bliss.

The buzzing beneath my skin subsides as I relax into the seat, and I also take the opportunity to study his profile. He's good-looking in a hooded-eye, full-lipped kind of way, I'll give him that. The line of his jaw is particularly attractive. I follow the line down to his throat, to his Adam's apple bobbing over the top of his open shirt collar. You can just about see the angry pink line where I scratched him.

That mark.

It's mine.

"Getting a good look, are we?" he drawls.

"How did you get that scar?" I shift my gaze to stare right at it. I can't help it. I want to have that connection with him. The void in me demands it.

His jaw tightens and the playfulness that was there only moments ago fades from his face. "Fucking. How else?"

"Delightful," I say. "She must have been worth it."

"Worth every second."

His words make me smile.

Finally, we reach my road.

"So, this is where you live, Tory." He pulls up outside, the soft hum of the engine purring. As he runs a hand through his dark hair, he gives the outside of my house a cursory glance. It's probably a dangerous thing…letting a serial killer-slash-target see where you live, even temporarily.

It gives me a rush. I don't know why.

"You're not coming in," I remind him. I've no clue what the etiquette is around these things, but fuck all that. I'm not having him in my house.

He gives me a smirk. It looks forced. "I wouldn't dream of it…"

I roll my eyes and unclip my belt, ready to leave. "I'll see you tomorrow."

"Because we can finish what you started right here," he says in a low voice.

His words make me pause. Lorcan uses my hesitation to unclip his seatbelt in one smooth action and leans over, filling the space around me with his woody, citrusy scent. His hand takes me by the throat, thumb pressing on the soft fleshy part to stop me from leaving.

I jerk back as his lips graze mine, but he forces his way inside. His lips are soft, but the kiss is brutal. For a brief moment, I sink into it, letting his teeth and tongue fill the void in me that's been building from the moment I walked out of Dante's cabin.

But it doesn't last. *It never fucking lasts.*

Without thinking, I bite down hard until I taste blood, for no other reason than I need to. I'm waiting for Lorcan to pull back and accuse me of being a bitch, or to hit me. He doesn't. He hisses and carries on, devouring me, trapping me against the soft leather seat.

At that, my mind flies to dangerous places.

What else can I do to him?

I'm only half-aware that his hand is yanking open my school shirt to grope my breasts. Then he's under my super short skirt tearing the soaking wet strip of my knickers away with his fingers. He slips a finger inside. The moan comes out of my mouth before I can stop it.

"Fuck. Tory. You're soaking wet," he says, mauling at the silk and lace. "Take these off or I will…"

No…

Fuck. My dagger is under my skirt.

I grab his hand, digging my nails in. "Get the fuck off me." I pry him away.

Lorcan grunts and pulls back, eyes dark and devious. The smirk on his lips isn't pretty. "I see. You don't like not being in control."

"Don't do that again, or fucking follow me," I say, scowling, opening the door to his rich wanker car.

I slip out of the Bugatti as Lorcan chuckles. He watches me go, massively turned on if the bulge in his trousers is anything to go by. Heart pounding, letting me know I'm alive, I slam the fucking door in his face.

I make it to my house without him coming after me.

His car roars off into the distance as I step inside, shaking, but not from desire or embarrassment. I'm fucking annoyed. Adrenaline is ransacking my body. I let my guard down. Lorcan isn't just my target…

He's a fucking teenager. I should know better.

If I don't, I'm just as bad as the men I kill. *Even worse.*

I lock the door and pause, blinking at my appearance in the hallway mirror. I'm startled by my blood-flushed cheeks, swollen lips, and disheveled state. My eyes are wide as saucers. And even a strand of pale blonde is peeking out from beneath my fake brown waves.

Shit.

In the heat of it all, I forgot I was wearing a wig.

As soon as I get into my bedroom, I strip off the awful uniform and the wig and take another long, cold shower. The freezing cold jets of water raw against my skin reminds me that I'm alive, waking me out of whatever daze recent events seem to have put me in.

After I've washed, I sit at my kitchen table with an Italian microwave meal, my hair still dripping wet, working through my target's file as I eat.

Somehow, he got my number and sent me a message.

Let's do that again sometime.

I read it over and over again. I don't know how to reply so I don't bother.

I mean, what do I say. I'm no good at this shit.

There's also a new message from Quinn asking me to drop by as soon as I can, and a message from Polina asking if I've made any 'fucking progress'.

I don't bother to call her back. I updated her yesterday after I got home. She's a fucking idiot if she thinks I'd have anything to tell her after one day. And I'm definitely not telling her that I nearly screwed the target.

Because the truth is, I wanted Lorcan in the car. I've been wanting it since I saw him chained up in that sex club, covered in the slashes I gave him.

I should probably kill him before I give into that need. I should take the heat still plaguing my body, and funnel it into something I can use.

Rage.

Pictures of Aurora's body as it was found, in sharp, unadulterated contrast to her school portrait, lay scattered around me.

I look at them until the images are burnt into my memory. I take notes and eat my spaghetti. Until I can't seem to let go of my fork.

Every bruise. Every cut. Every bite…

She was destroyed.

And she was only seventeen.

It claws at some dark part of my soul to see it, slithering under my skin like a well-known grudge. A buzzing in my brain, fogging everything else out, hungers for violence on her behalf. If the guy who did this was standing before me right now, I would take my fork and ram it through his eye socket straight into his pathetic lizard brain.

And it would feel *so* right.

THIRTEEN

VIOLA

DUKE IS WAITING in the crowded hallway where my locker is on Wednesday morning.

A dark thrill runs down my spine as our eyes meet. He cocks his head, giving me a strange look. *Still trying to figure me out, Duke? Try harder.*

Someone shouts over to him. "Lor, are you coming?"

We both look to our left and down the end of the hallway. It's Finlay Baron with his dirty-blond hair and permanent sneer plastered on his face. Lorcan, ignoring his friend, flicks his gaze back to me.

He looks me up and down, eye fucking every inch. "You didn't reply to my message."

I toss my hair. "No, I didn't."

"Why the fuck not?"

"I was busy. And it wasn't a question."

"Cagey little bitch, aren't you?" he says, stepping closer.

I don't move or take a step back. I stand my ground as he comes close enough that I can see the gold flecks in his green eyes. They peer down into mine, searching for answers.

He's so close I can smell the shower gel he used this morning, and the woodsy scent of his cologne.

Adrenaline surges in my veins. The busy corridor falls away. It's the dark room in the night club all over again.

It's just Duke and me.

Alone

This is what hunting is all about.

"Lorcan, are you coming?" Finn asks, his presence swarming into view, ruining the moment I have with my prey. Finn looks at me like I'm dinner. I look at him like he's trash. He frowns and tears his gaze away, rounding on his friend. "We're going to be late."

A storm clouds over in Duke's eyes. "Piss off, Finn. Can't you see I'm busy."

"We're going to be late for the vote," Finn huffs, shooting me a dark look.

"Not anymore," says Lorcan dismissively. "I called it off."

Finn glares at Lorcan. "What the fuck? Why?"

"I told you, I'm out." Lorcan looks at me with hooded eyes. "You're coming to my party on Saturday." It's a statement, not a question.

"Yes, I already said I would. With Dino."

"Not with Dino, with me," Lorcan adds.

"Do I get a say in this?" I ask, tilting my head.

Lorcan smiles, it doesn't reach his shark-like eyes. "No, you don't, sweetheart. I'll pick you up at six. Wear something tight."

I'm not surprised to see Dino waiting for me after class the next day. I've had two of them accost me this week, why not a third?

Dino. When did I start calling him Dino?

"Tory, a few of us are heading to the boathouse. Want to come with?"

"To do what?" I say.

"Drink, get fucked."

"It's Wednesday night?"

"No one bothers with class on Thursday. It's sports day."

"Who's going?"

"The usual. The Dukes, Baron, the Astors. Cecilia might drop by after music practice. She's not been well these past few days so she might go home early again."

I shrug. I do need to have a word with Cecilia, if she shows up. It could also be the perfect opportunity to spy on my target some more. The more I get to know him, the easier my job will be to make it look like an accident. I need to call Quinn, but I can do that later.

He goes to throw his arm around me. I step back, narrowly avoiding his embrace. The hurt look on his face says it all. Not that I know what to do about that. I get that he wants me to show him some affection, but I'm already talking to him more than any other guy in this damn school, my target included. *Why isn't that enough?*

Deep down, I know the answer.

I've studied enough human behavior to know when I see it.

Dino is a fucking hugger.

Outside, the sun has started to set. As we walk to the lamp-lit leafy pathway that leads to the boathouse, I dig into my limited energy reserves, allowing a smile and Dino to walk closer to me than I would generally like. Not because I don't want to hurt his feelings, or that I feel bad.

I don't feel anything.

I'm supposed to be playing the part of a 'normal' teenager. I'm supposed to seduce the guy. Dante's words echo in my mind. It's time I started doing my fucking job. The host of messages on my phone from Polina are a testament to that fact.

I should've killed Lorcan already. At least I know how I'm going to do it. I gave Polina the update last night. She was less than pleased but relieved to know it's all going to be over soon.

The familiar spike of excitement before a kill doesn't spear through me like it usually does. Instead, my skin itches, like it's too tight over my bones.

I feel strange.

I must *look* strange because Vice glances over and gives me a hesitant look.

"What?"

"Are you okay?"

"I'm fine."

"You look like you're plotting the end of the world."

My mask must be slipping if he can see as much as that in my face. I let my features become unreadable before I look over at him. I'm just in time to see him reach out and then stop, curling his hand into a fist and then dropping it.

"You don't like me touching you, do you?"

"I hate people," I say with honesty, surprising myself.

"How so?" Dino asks, sounding genuinely interested.

I shift my gaze to him. He even looks interested.

Okay. I'll admit, there's something about talking to Vice that doesn't fill me with unease afterward, like showing the real me behind the mask. Whatever I've said or done around him so far hasn't had him sneering or recoiling in horror.

It's refreshing for someone who has to constantly hide what she is...*if nothing else.*

"I don't enjoy being with others," I say after a pause.

He runs his hands through his hair, shooting a worried look in my direction. "Shit. Did something...happen, to make you like this?"

"No. I was just born this way. Everyone always thinks I'm damaged, but the truth is, I would be if nature hadn't given me what I needed, or lack of need, to survive."

There I go again, spouting my mouth off to fucking Dino. How does he have this hold over me? *Who is this boy?*

I utter a soft curse under my breath and look his way. My body suddenly tense, ready.

But all he does is nod, looking relieved. "So, what about sex?"

"What about it?"

"Does your 'not enjoying others' thing mean you're a virgin?" he asks, sounding a little too fucking hopeful.

I snort. "Fuck no. Sex is different. I like *that*. It's useful."

The look on his face is amused, and for a minute I don't understand it until he speaks. "Useful. That's not how I'd describe it."

We walk for a bit longer in silence until the dickhead stops and turns to face me, making me halt. His eyes are softly focused, his breathing slow. "So, you're okay if I do this?"

He steps closer.

If he kisses me, I'll bite his fucking tongue off.

He leans in, lips brushing mine. His tongue darts out to taste me. For the barest second, I don't move. I'm rigid fucking stone. His breath is warm, and he smells like citrus and cinnamon.

He doesn't kiss me. Instead, he bites my lip, hard, drawing a moan from somewhere inside of me. A rush sweeps up from my core. It soothes the ache that Lorcan left behind after he blind-sided me in his car.

"Or if I take you here in the woods, in the dark. Would you like that?" His voice is pure silk, a caress on the wind. Nothing harsh. Nothing brutal. Just plain seduction that I'm not ready for. His eyes are devilish looking in the low light.

Dino is not the kitten I thought he was.

Oh no you fucking don't.

I shove him off me and push past him, carrying on walking. My breathing is harsher, quicker. I may not feel emotions the same way as others, but my body betrays me every second it can. Fucking biology.

"You need to work on your personal space," I say after a breath, as I glance back over my shoulder. *All the boys at Sacred Heart bloody need to.*

It's so dark now, I can barely see Dino. But I know he's fucking grinning.

Dammit.

If I'm not careful, this job, this school, these boys…will blow up in my face.

Music blares and there are students drinking and hooking up everywhere at the boathouse. A group of them lounging on the indoor seating area look up as we walk in through the entrance way.

Dino grabs two beers from the fridge, and then leads me out onto the dock where the usual crowd are hanging. He plonks himself down on the decking steps facing the lake, pats his lap and offers me a beer.

I'm not a fucking lap dog, but I don't say that or let it show. The look I give him is unreadable as I take off my blazer, despite the cold, and grab the beer, and lower myself onto my jacket to sit beside him. Light is falling rapidly as I glance around and take in the faces.

Two guys amidst a gaggle of girls a few steps down with hazel eyes and hair to match, flash teeth as they take me in simultaneously. They lift their drink at Dino, and he raises his in return.

"Harley and Henry Astor, heirs to the Astor motor empire and family fortune," Dino whispers in my ear before taking a chug of his beer. "And total fuckboys, if you haven't noticed already." I already know this, but I nod and drink a mouthful with him.

The others in the group haven't spoken or even looked at me or Dino. Finn is dead center with his arm around Carly, drinking what looks to be hard liquor. He flashes me a look that I can only describe as carnal. Saskia, talking in a low voice to her friend, glances up.

Lorcan is nowhere to be seen.

"Why is she here?" Saskia gives Dino a scathing look. "When I allowed you back in here, I never said you could bring the trash with you."

"This isn't your fucking boathouse, Saskia," Dino cuts in.

"I think you'll find that my father owns most of this school, so yes I think it is. Who is she anyway? A nobody."

"Oh, piss off, Saskia, no one gives a fuck," Dino says, voice a little strained. He looks at me. "Ignore her. I've learnt to."

I take a swig of my drink and look out at the lake. Ignoring them all, even the way Dino leans close. His teasing earlier has thrown me off my game. He's a student, younger than me by a good number of years. Lorcan too.

I can't put my finger on what it is about either of them that draws me in.

Whatever it is though my rules are clear.

I don't fuck targets. And I sure as hell don't take advantage of horny schoolboys, even if they are legal. Knowing where the lines are keeps me from getting caught. I need them like I need to breathe. Because without them, I'll go fucking nuclear, and the one person I'm trying to stay hidden from will know where I am.

That can't happen.

My father can't find me.

Ever.

There's a commotion inside. I look over my shoulder to see Lorcan and Jude walking out onto the deck with three girls I've never seen before, all of them seemingly pissed as newts.

Jude notices me first. His brow furrows but then he turns back to the girl practically hanging off him. She takes his hand and slips it down the front of her blouse. He grins and yanks her toward him, groping her ass as he leers. It doesn't take them long to both disappear off into the boathouse. I don't know why that makes me want to frown but it does.

Strange reaction to have.

Lorcan steers the other two drunken girls over to the rest of us. It's not hard to notice his shirt hanging loose, his tie rammed in his pocket, and a smear of lipstick on his neck. The sight of it leaves a bitter taste in my mouth.

I'm still frowning when he catches me looking, staring at me with those cold, lifeless eyes of his. My heart beats a little louder in my fucking chest. As he leaves the girls with the others and walks over to where I'm sitting with Dino, his eyes raze down to pin me where I sit. Mouth dry, still bitter, I take a swig of my beer to wash it all away.

At the last moment, his eyes flick to Dino. "A word inside." He doesn't say anything else but turns and walks into the boathouse.

FOURTEEN

DINO

I CAN'T BE FUCKED with this. I get to my feet. Tory arches a brow but says nothing.

"I won't be a minute."

She looks up at me with those big blue eyes. "What do you think he wants?"

"Fuck knows. It's Lorcan," I say by way of explanation.

Inside the boathouse, Duke is lounging on the middle sofa, one ankle perched across his knee, the epitome of patience. Finn is on the other sofa, knocking back a beer.

Last night, I thought Jude was going to kill him just for being the prick he is. I know they sorted things out, both of them appearing in the boathouse fucked out of their minds says that, but not to what degree.

"Are we back on? What's this about?" I ask.

Duke eyes me like he's fucking sick of me asking that. But what does he expect, no one knows what's in his fucking mind. He just does shit and expects us all to deal with the mess afterward.

I'm so fucking tired of his bullshit.

That goes for Marques too. *Where the hell is he, anyway?*

In answer to my question, moaning and banging reverberates from the closed door across the open hallway. Chuckling, I take position against the wall across from Lorcan, so we're both facing the bathroom listening to the sounds of Jude fucking some poor girl up against the toilet cubicle door.

Less than ten minutes later, the moans stop, and Jude emerges, eyes wild, a dusting of white under his nose. Not far behind, the girl who was all over him outside, appears too, disheveled with her skirt hitched up, and completely fucking wasted. She sees us both and exits quickly, leaving the four of us alone.

Jude rearranges his pants and then staggers into the kitchen to get a beer. When he returns, the look Lorcan is giving him could strip fucking paint.

"What?" Jude exclaims.

"Have you quite finished?"

"Oh, fuck you, Duke, and your holier than thou bullshit." He leans against the wall, eyes flitting between the two of us. After a moment, they settle on me.

Lorcan is glaring at me too so I know something is up. Finn is all evil smiles.

"Why are you all looking at me like that?" I say.

"Did you find out?" Lorcan asks, cocking a brow.

"I fucking knew it," I stand up ready to leave.

Lorcan motions for me to sit down. I hesitate to jump like a little bitch, but I know when and when not to push Lorcan to the limit.

I sit back down, scowling.

I narrow my eyes. "Has this got something to do with you missing the vote?"

"Fuck the vote. We've already decided," says Jude.

We usually vote on this shit, as a group. Lorcan and Jude deciding together is not how this works.

I get to my feet. "This is a fucking joke."

"Sit the fuck down, I'm not finished yet," Lorcan snarls.

"Why her?" I demand, not sitting down.

He shrugs. "Why the fuck not?"

"She's not like the others. Not this one."

"There's no one else. We need an elite bitch as bait to make this work."

"Then we use one of the others."

"Everyone's paid their dues. We're out of fresh fucking meat. You know that."

"Then why do it anymore. Just tell them to go fuck themselves."

Lorcan arches a brow at Jude as if to say 'see, I fucking told you'.

"We have a system. You fuck with the system and one of the girls pays the price. Cecilia pays the price. Saskia pays the price," Jude tones at me. "You want it to be Sas next?"

I shake my head. "No, but I don't want Tory to be part of this either. Leave her out of it."

"No can do. Those Norton Priory bitches are giving us the run around. There's no one else."

I dart a look over my shoulder. Tory is sitting where I left her, drinking her beer. She's gazing out onto the lake completely oblivious.

This is fucked up. There has to be another fucking way.

Lorcan clears his throat. "Sinner," he says, using the nickname from when we were kids. He drops his leg and leans forward. "It's a simple question. Answer it. Did you fucking find out?"

"She's not a virgin," I snap, turning back to the room.

He leans back, looking satisfied. "Good. It's better if she's not."

"What I want to know is, are we sharing this one, or is Sinner breaking her in all by himself?" Finn pipes up, finally adding his two cents.

"Fuck. That's all you think about, isn't it, Shitboy. Getting your bloody dick wet," I scoff at him.

He shrugs. "The girls like it better when you ease them in.

Plus, she's fucking hot. We should tap that ass before the old bastards do."

The sneer is on my face before I can stop it. "They're not touching her. No one is. You fucking touch her, Finn, and you're fucking dead."

Jude shakes his head. "Remember the reason we're doing this."

I glare at him. "We usually give them a choice."

"She'll get her choice. She can come to the party, or she can stay at home and miss out on all the fun," Lorcan adds.

"This is fucking sick." I shake my head.

"No," says Lorcan as he gets to his feet. "It's good business. Just make sure she understands the consequences."

"Fucking bullshit," is all I have to say about that.

Jude's eyes narrow as he straightens up, posturing like the fucking prick he is. "She's a fucking senior. We ALL make sacrifices. Even her."

Lorcan's face is unreadable. "He's not wrong. We've all made them. All of us. What makes her so fucking special?" he adds.

"We've all made sacrifices? What about Sas? When is she going to make them?" I snarl at him. "Because I don't see you asking your cunt of a sister to spread her legs."

Finn gives a low whistle. "Below the belt, mate."

Lorcan blinks at me and for a second, I think he's going to snap and actually kill me. After the longest minute, he comes up close.

"I'll give you that one because my sister did a number on you. But the next time you disrespect her, I'll carve your broken heart from your fucking chest and feed it to the fishes in your mother's fucking koi-carp pond." His eyes are shining as he says it.

Lor means every word.

Then he exhales and stalks—hands in pockets—out of the room and back to the party.

It's Jude who comes up to me next, shaking his head. "Sas has enough to deal with at home. You of all people should fucking know that."

"Everything okay?" Tory looks up in askance as I come out of the boathouse. She inclines her head, her penetrating gaze ripping into my fucking soul.

I fucking hate this.

"Come on, let's go. Lor said you didn't have a car. I'll give you a ride home."

"No, you won't. I'm taking her," says Lorcan, coming over, keys in hand.

Tory glances between the two of us. "Fucking idiots," she sighs under her breath. "Either one of you will do." And she strides off into the darkness leaving us both standing there.

Lorcan arches a brow, and then looks at me as I open my mouth to speak. "Your bike is a fucking deathtrap. I'm taking her," he says.

And then he disappears off into the night after Tory, while his sister shoots me evils like it's all my damned fault.

Fuck this shit.

FIFTEEN

VIOLA

"HEY, YOU," Saskia's scornful gaze takes me in the next day as I stand in just a towel and nothing else. "Vickie, is it?"

I give her a blank look and then head towards my things.

I'm not at all surprised to see Saskia and her sidekick, Carly, standing in the middle of the girls' changing rooms after hockey practice.

"Why is Lorcan taking an interest in you?" Her cold voice cuts through the girl-chatter.

Interest is an understatement. "That's none of your business," I say, without flourish.

"He's family, so I think it is my business."

"Good for you," I say, getting dressed.

She crosses her arms and tilts her head. "You're not his type so don't waste your breath. They're just using you. They've done it to all the girls. You're nothing special."

"I honestly couldn't care less right now," I sigh.

There are a few titters, but mostly the room is silent.

The feral look Saskia gives me is reminiscent of her brother,

129

but not quite. She's more fire than ice. I wonder how both siblings, only a year apart, developed such different ways of coping.

"Dino's going to be disappointed you're ditching him for my brother," she sneers.

"Who said I'm ditching Dino?" I say. "Maybe I'll go with both of them."

She narrows her eyes at me. "What kind of slut are you?"

"One that can handle more than one cock," I say absently, untying the band around the length of my wig. I should have dyed my hair. It would have been easier.

"You admit it, you're a fucking whore?" She smirks. "Finn was right about you. You'll fit right in at the party. There are plenty of cocks to go around there."

I give her a shrug, not really looking at her. I hear her talking but her words mean nothing. "Who gives a fuck. Why are you so interested? Jealous your ex doesn't want you anymore? Or that I can fuck your brother without breaking the law?" I ask in a level voice. "Because you seem awfully interested in your brother's cock."

Maybe I should dye it?

Saskia's face turns bright red as her jaw clenches.

"Just stay away from *our* boys, *Vickie*, or you'll fucking regret it." Saskia stalks out of the changing room.

"You have a fucking death wish," Carly snarls, and stalks after her, leaving me in peace to get changed.

If I wanted to slip in and out of this school unnoticed, it's never going to happen now. In less than a week, Lorcan driving me home twice, and Saskia's little changing room episode has put me on the student map. Everyone seems to know who I am and that I've somehow caught the unwanted attention of the heirs to London's biggest crime syndicate—The Dukes.

Open season comes to mind.

Girls whisper when I'm not looking. Boys openly make lewd comments. By Friday afternoon my locker is stuffed completely full of condoms, and the word 'whore' is scrawled all over my things in permanent marker. Some joker even thought it would be hilarious to cut the crotch out of my swimsuit, and my running shorts, right before my sports classes.

But the most original has to be someone pretending to be the school nurse asking me to come to the clinic over the tannoy, much to the delight of the entire student body, because someone informed them that I may have an STD and need a check-up.

In another life, as a normal teenager, these little pranks might have got to me. I'm far from upset. I've endured much worse. Compared to my actual school, this place is a goddamn holiday camp.

At lunchtime, I get a message from Polina. I text her back that I don't have an update. I also get a voicemail from Dante asking me if I need any help since it's been almost two weeks already. I send him a reply back that it's going to plan and to back the fuck off. I know him. Dante doesn't believe in helping others. He has another agenda, like getting a cut of the fee.

I don't need him. I can't even be bothered asking him for a car anymore.

I have it all under control.

Students gossiping and eating, sitting in groups, flick their gaze at me as I enter the cafeteria through the double swinging doors. I take my lunch tray over to one of the empty tables and sit down. As I give an unruffled look across the room, they duck their heads and whisper amongst themselves.

"That's the new girl. She's only been here one week and already she's fucking both Dino and Lorcan."

"Both of them? What a slut."

"Total whore."

My jaw ticks as I listen to their shitty gossip. It doesn't bode well that I'm already the object of fucking drama.

So much for undercover.

Across the room, there's a commotion as the Dukes walk in with, Jude, Dino and Carly. Dino is the first one to shoot me an apologetic look. Saskia gives me a scornful one. Jude frowns my way. Lorcan ignores me completely.

I refocus on my laptop just as some dickhead schoolboy decides to throw something at me. It hits my chin and falls down, leaving a wet smear, landing in my dessert.

It's a used condom.

Calmly, I push my dessert away.

All around, there's an explosion of laughter. *Fucking kids. Do they not have anything better to do?* It's tiring how much energy I have to expend not to do some permanent fucking damage. This job is seriously beginning to grate on me.

Dino, of all people, breaks away from the group and places his tray on my table. The titters die out to nothing. I'm not sure whether to react to the condom, the dubious stain on my chin, or his shitty company first.

"Have mine," he says, exchanging my dessert bowl for his.

I disregard his peace offering. I'm not really a sweet-tooth person. The clean freak in me wants to shower, the savage in me wants to stab someone in the eye. I stare at the schoolboy who threw the disgusting thing. He's posturing, getting respect from the guys around him.

Finlay *fucking* Baron.

"Ignore him, he's just doing what Saskia tells him to do. Here." Dino reaches into his blazer pocket and offers me a clean tissue.

I shoot a dark look at Dino. He's being too nice. It's annoying as hell. I want to ask him where he's been all day. He's usually hovering around, but after Lorcan drove me home last night Dino has been keeping away. Did Lorcan say something to him, or was it Saskia? If so, why does that bother me so much.

There's a scraping of chairs as Finn's table disperses. Finn sneers at me as he gets to his feet. One of his dickhead friends high-fives him while Saskia gives him a nod of approval.

Absolute fucking sons of bitches.

I relax my shoulders, pick up my eating knife, and calmly stand up.

Dino frowns. "Where are you going?"

"For a walk," I say. "Stay. I won't be a minute."

I follow Finn out of the school dining room, down one of the side corridors, and into a bathroom. He's pissing when I walk in.

"Hey... what are you—" I stalk over and grab his pathetic cock mid-piss and twist it, making his eyes bulge. He screams beautifully. I ram the blunt end of the knife up against his groin and pull his dick so hard, it forces him to his knees.

I crouch down so we're at eye level. "If you ever do that again, I will cut this shitty excuse for a knob off. Understand?"

He nods, unable to speak, eyes misting up.

"Good boy." I pat him on the cheek with my piss-covered hand. "Now get yourself together. Come back to my table, and eat your fucking mess."

I wash my hands and clean my face, and then walk back to the cafeteria. I take my seat opposite Dino. His dessert is mostly melted, but I pull it toward me and eat a spoonful, just as a disheveled Finlay Baron comes limping back in. He doesn't even look at me as he picks up my ice cream bowl with the condom on top of it. He takes it to an empty table and starts eating. The whole room is silent as he does.

Dino is looking at me with wonder in his eyes. Saskia appears confused. Jude is just outright frowning.

Lorcan though, he's struggling not to laugh. His mouth is twitching, almost curling up into a snarl. Our eyes meet, and he gives me a look that makes me want to kill him more than once.

I don't acknowledge his approval. I turn away and carry on

eating my fucking ice cream. Dino's eyes are burning holes in the side of my head.

"Are you here at Saskia's bidding too, Vice?" I finally ask him, just because I can't take him looking at me like he is a second longer.

He holds his hands up. "Hey, no. Not me."

"Then tell me who spread the rumors?"

"It definitely wasn't me."

I blink at him. "Did you un-spread them?"

"No," he says after a pause, his Adam's apple bobbing up and down.

"Then you're just as bad," I say, rolling my eyes. I know why he's here. It was easy enough, and low-lit around the boathouse, to slip my earpiece in and listen to the boys' entire conversation. Not that it made much sense. But I get the impression they want me to do something for them at this infamous party of theirs.

I'll go to the party.

But my reason for going is very different from theirs.

Very different.

"Tory, I'm sor—"

"Just make it up to me and tell me where this fucking party is going to be."

He sucks in a breath, unable to look at me. "About that. I can't take you tomorrow. Lorcan wants to do it and to be honest, I don't think you should go. They use girls to…" He shakes his head as though he can't believe what he's saying. "…smooth over business deals."

"You said it would be fine if I wasn't single."

"Lorcan's not buying that. If you go—"

"I'm going. And I don't need either of you to take me. I can go by myself."

"That's not how it works."

"You think I give a shit?"

He frowns and leans back. "No. I don't think you do." He shifts his gaze over at Saskia giving us both evils, and then at

Lorcan ignoring the room like he's above it. *The boy is fucking whipped.*

"Send me the address," I say as I get to my feet. There's only so much joy I can get out of sitting in a school canteen, pretending to eat a bowl of watery cream. "Or I'll show you what I did to Baron to make him eat his own cum."

SIXTEEN

VIOLA

THE ADDRESS DINO sent me is hardly the secret location I was expecting. It's the Duke's family residence on Rosebury Drive.

I pull up outside in my Beetle and check my make-up in the mirror. I'm wearing clothes I don't mind getting fucked up—a black jersey dress, black boots, and a leather jacket. I'm wearing my silver jewelry to soften the look. This is supposed to be a party after all.

Lorcan wanted tight.

This is as tight as I'm prepared to go.

My phone buzzed on the way over here. It's Dante again, being extra attentive. I don't like it. He needs to butt out of my fucking business.

I stare at my phone, reading the last of Dante's messages, and it rings in my hand.

"I'm doing it tonight. I'm at his house," I tell Polina. Why is she constantly on my back?

"I want to know as soon as it's done. Don't make me fucking have to chase you for it, or I'll make this job your last."

She hangs up.

Her threat doesn't bother me. What does, is that I'm wasting time on this job when I could be onto the next one. The fee Polina paid me has nearly all gone, most of it on the mundane—accountant's bills, weapon suppliers, expenses. The rest on making sure I'm not caught or ever found.

Because I can't go back.

I reach down and double-check the hidden vial of opiate cocktail is inside my boot. My plan is to slip him the drugs, hide until he passes out, and then stick an overdose in his veins and a pillow over his head. It's far cleaner than faking suicide by shooting, hanging, or even drowning. I just need to check a few things which I couldn't verify at school, so as not to raise any unnecessary questions…

Like, does Lorcan Duke still get shit-faced on drugs?

I'm pulled out of my thoughts by a sports bike roaring onto the driveway. Training my sights on the plate in the dark, I recognize Dino's Ducati. His personal plate V1 ICE is unmistakable.

I was right to bring my own car. I will not be stranded here after killing a target, and there's no way I'm perching on the back of a fucking bike when I'm not the one in control. No fucking way.

I get out of my Beetle just as Dino is taking his helmet off.

He gives me a sheepish look, securing his helmet on the back of his bike seat. "Heads up. Lorcan's pissed. He waited for you and you didn't show."

I give him a blank look. "So?"

He grins. "You just don't give a fuck, do you?"

"No. Why would I? It's a waste of time."

And I already knew. I slipped a tracking bug into Lorcan's car yesterday evening when he kindly gave me a lift home. Quinn's tracking app showed him waiting outside the school for about thirty minutes before giving up.

I'd already left but it was fun to see how long he'd stay.

I walk to the front door and Dino joins me, casually draping one arm around me as we enter. I let him. It's going to look like Dino brought me here and severely piss Lorcan off even more.

I couldn't have timed it better if I'd tried.

As we traipse through the elegant, rich wanker mansion, there are teens in various stages of inebriation, I recognize a few of them from school. Some are sitting on the sofas, dancing to the loud music, or making out already. A select few are crowding around in the pool in the summer room, screaming, laughing, flirting, spilling onto the lawn through bi-folding doors.

"You're not like anyone I've ever met," Dino says as he guides me into the house, hand around my waist like he owns me. My skin itches where his fingers lightly trace. I have a certain tolerance for unwanted touching—Dino is brushing the edge of that tolerance by a hair's breadth. I suppress the urge to make him bleed as Lorcan watches us from his position beside the pool.

Lorcan.

Inside my chest, my heart is trying to climb out of it. My nerves are playing havoc with my focus, sending it off in all different directions. I'm wound tight and it probably shows. I may not feel emotion, but my body has absolutely no qualms with fucking up my life. If I could take drugs and be done with these shitty responses, I would.

My soon-to-be-dead target takes a swig of his glass, finishing his drink of something dark, disregarding me with one last look of his arrogant eyes before turning away. He gestures to a girl, whispers something in her ear, and sends her off towards the kitchen.

"Do you want a drink?" Dino asks. *Yes. I fucking need one.*

"I'll get it." I say to Dino, giving him a charming smile.

"Okay. Can you grab me a beer then?" He returns the smile, making small circles on my back which I tolerate. It's all for show.

"Just beer?"

"Trust me, you don't want to drink anything else at this party."

As I head toward the crowded kitchen, I flick a gaze at Duke, noting where he's standing and who he's with. Chuckling, humor never reaching his eyes, he says something to his posse—Jude Marques, one of the Astors, and Finn Baron. All but the latter shoot me a scornful glance. Finn, on the other hand, looks fucking terrified.

I give Finn a dark grin, making him splutter his mouthful of drink all over himself before averting his eyes.

One down, four to go.

Once inside the kitchen, I locate the drinks. The girl who Duke spoke to is carrying a bottle of whisky.

"Wait," I say. "Can I get a splash of that before you take it out to the boys?"

She nods, handing me the unopened bottle. I pull the top off and pour out a couple of fingers, adding ice and coke. I'm not even meant to be drinking, but fuck it. One won't hurt.

I hand it back to her.

Outside, Dino is waiting for me. I glance around, noting faces. I don't see Saskia or any girls from school. Just boys and several girls who look like they don't belong. From their cheap branded clothing, bad dye-jobs, and their local accents they're way out of their depth here. Most are stumbling around letting the guys from school grope up their skirts and down their tops. A couple of the girls, wasted out of their minds, take their clothes off and dive into the pool.

I drift my gaze back over to Lorcan and the others. The girl with the bottle of whisky is delivering it to him. I watch her top everyone up and then all of them take a mouthful.

Three down. One left.

"Who are all these people? I only recognize half of them," I say walking up to where Dino is standing.

"Local girls the boys picked up in town. We're meant to bring two each," he says taking the bottle I offer him.

"To smooth over business deals?"

He shrugs and knocks his beer back. "That's not til later. This is just a tradition the lads have. Girls are grateful to party with us,

140

the boys get laid. Makes things easier if there's more pussy than less, if you know what I mean?"

No. I don't. Fucking weird tradition. "Where's your two? Couldn't fit them on your bike?"

"Girls from Sacred Heart or any of the elite schools count for extra."

"You didn't bring me though."

He grins. "They don't know that. And we're leaving as soon as this place heats up. Once everyone is fucked, they won't notice if we leave early."

I roll my eyes and slug my drink back. Whatever Dino's intention is tonight, he's not going to succeed. I need to do this quickly and then get out as fast as possible. Dino takes another slug of his beer, ingesting the opiates I spiked his drink with like a pro.

Good boy.

Movement in the corner of my eye makes me look up. Lorcan is leaving the group, going off on his own. Some drunk girl calls over to him, but he acts like he doesn't see or hear her and carries on into the house.

Fuck. I lost him.

I make my excuses to Dino that I need to find the bathroom, and head off into the house after Duke.

Lorcan's house is huge which gives me the perfect excuse to get lost in it. But I've no idea where my target is. He's only fucking disappeared. Still, he can't be far. If he leaves, the app on my phone connected to the tracker on his car will let me know. He's in this goddamn house somewhere.

Not that I'm looking for him. I need to find his bedroom first.

Once I'm up the grand staircase, I start looking inside rooms. Some of them have couples or more than that fucking in them already. Well, the guys are fucking...the girls look mostly passed out. Dino said to avoid drinking. It makes me wonder if the party of the evening, before the business side of things starts, is just some rape fest for these jocks to prey on girls who don't know any better or are too poor to do anything about it.

At least Dino told me not to come tonight. He gets brownie points for that, and for still trying to rescue me. He was following me here for a reason tonight. Poor guy.

Lorcan on the other hand…

He's just a fucking asshole.

It takes some searching, but I find Lorcan's bedroom on the third floor on the east side of the house. I know it's his because it's neat as fuck and there are sports trophies with his name on them all over the wall. The room is large with eaves on both sides and an extra-large king-size bed with black sheets in the center of it.

I slip on a pair of gloves and close the door behind me softly as lights blaze into the room. *Headlights? Has someone else just arrived?*

I pad over to the window to look out.

Down below, two black SUVs pile into the gated courtyard. Two distinguished men slightly drunk with smiles on their faces, two men in black suits that look like security guards, and a woman in one of those hideous pants suits, get out. I can't see their faces much, but the drunk men are definitely in the mature category. They don't look like parents, but their appearance screams rich and powerful, and corrupt. I deal with people like this every day. I know these types. They're not here for the good of their health.

One of them looks up—the woman.

I jerk back into the darkness.

I calm my breathing and still my reflexes. She didn't see me, but now is not the time to ride the adrenaline wave. I'll need that for later. I don't really care who Lorcan's guests are. Whoever they are, they were invited for his shady business transaction, and that just makes me want to end Lorcan's life that little bit more.

Methodically, I search his room, looking in all the usual places. I find a few strange things like a girl's diary and a lock of hair. But the final verdict is that Lorcan Duke doesn't do drugs anymore. The most he has are a few packets of vitamins in his bathroom cabinet. This guy is too fucking clean these days. What happened to him? He was a cokehead at fourteen the last time around.

In my jacket pocket are bottles of illegal painkillers. I slipped some into his locker before I left school, and now I add a few more to his bathroom cabinet tucked behind the mouthwash. I also throw an empty bottle in the wastebasket next to his desk.

The moment I walk out of this place, Quinn will insert a fake paper trail onto his laptop and anyone looking will see evidence of a Vicodin addiction and nothing more.

My phone buzzes in my pocket. I shove the diary and the lock of hair in my jacket, take my gloves off with a snap and then take my phone out. It's Dino worrying, looking for me. I text him a message to say I'll be back shortly since everything is going to plan.

"Tory, what are you doing?"

The world grinds to a halt as I look up and see Lorcan Duke watching me from the doorway in the room I didn't even know was there.

Duke. You sneaky little fuck.

"I was looking for the bathroom," I say, offhandedly, heart racing like crazy in my chest the second I see the glint in his eyes that doesn't bode well.

He cocks his head. "You were?" He steps through the hidden door and closes it. "I don't believe you. I think you knew this was my room," he says with a silken voice. "You've been playing games with me since day one."

Adrenaline rages through my veins.

"Why would I do that?" I say, unmoving, trying to regain control of my breathing.

He smiles, a dark one full of dark promises, and stalks over until he's towering above me. His pupils are large and unfocused. "It was you the other night, wasn't it?"

Okay, Viola, how do you get out of this one?

My hand hovers over where my dagger is beneath the material

of my dress. "I've no idea what you're talking about," I say, taking a step back.

I could stab him with my dagger. He might be bigger, taller, and weighs about 180 pounds, but he won't fucking see that coming. The only issue with that is that it wouldn't be an accident. I'd have to disappear for good. Polina doesn't accept mistakes. She erases them.

Lorcan paces closer, swaying slightly, looking at me like I'm prey and he's the carnivore. At that thought, a thrill shoots down through me, giving me goosebumps.

Hunting carnivores is my favorite

I could also just wait until the drugs I slipped into his whisky kick in.

He grabs my chin, fingers digging in, and forces me against the bedpost. Pain flares as some wooden carving on the post digs into my spine. "Did you enjoy cutting me up?"

He's still quite strong for a drugged guy.

Instinctively, my hand flies to my dagger, but he catches my wrist before I can. He hauls and flips me onto the bed face down. Using his knee in the middle of my back, he pins me to the mattress so I can barely move, twisting my arms behind me. Shit, I should have seen this coming. It's a move I know because it's one I use a lot. There's no getting out of it. *How the hell does a rich prick schoolboy know fucking police disarming tactics?*

I feel his hand grope under my skirt and alleviate me of my dagger.

It clatters onto the floor as he tosses it across the room.

"I could do this all night, sweetheart," he drawls. "Now are you going to tell me the real reason you're stalking me?"

I turn my head to the side, breathing hard.

I'm so fucking angry, but I can't ignore the fact that I'm also fucking turned on.

It's been a long time since a guy managed to get the upper hand over me.

I observe that, shove it somewhere I don't have to fucking look at it, and steady my breathing while my mind thinks of all the ways to get out of this situation.

"I came here for you," I say, putting as much huskiness as I can into my already breathless voice.

He pushes his knee into my spine hard. "What do you mean?"

"Isn't it obvious? You came on to me in the car. Now I want more…"

"You came here to fuck?"

"Is that so hard to believe?"

He hesitates until there's a loud knock at the door. The hidden door.

"Fuck," he hisses. There's another knock, louder. He leans until his breath is hot on my neck, and whispers into my ear. "Get into the wardrobe. If you make a sound, I'll let them have you."

He lifts off, giving me enough room to sit up. His green eyes are searching in the low light, looking for lies and deceit. I show him the mask I've always lived behind and get off the bed, taking my time to walk over to the wardrobe. Or should I say a room with clothes in it? *Fucking rich people.*

I'm happy to note the room has an inside lock and a window. *If the shit hits the fan, at least I know my escape route.*

I close the door, but not all the way, and stare through the gap. My curiosity has always got me into trouble. I can't not walk the edge. Not because I enjoy the risk, but because I can. That's probably the only true thing I know about myself, I'll keep walking the line until I'm dead.

Lorcan goes over to the wall where the secret door is. On the way, he stops and picks up my dagger, and pockets it. Then he flicks on the lamp, making the room brighter, and presses a button on the side of the desk. The hidden door swings open. An older woman, late forties, the same woman who came in the SUV, is behind it.

She saunters into the room as though she owns it.

"You kept me waiting long enough."

"I was jerking off to a picture of your daughter. Didn't think you'd want to see that," Lorcan slurs.

She slaps him, the sound makes a loud crack in the room.

Lorcan doesn't retaliate but he looks fucking pissed.

"How is Sonia by the way? Send her my love," he chuckles, swaying hard, eyes huge and deadpan as he licks the blood on his lip.

She glares at him. "You're wasted. Fucking useless piece of shit."

"We did what you wanted," he shrugs.

"I wanted young girls of pedigree, not fucking trash whores," she snarls. She closes the gap and grabs him by the jaw, long nails digging in. "Maybe I should let them have you? Boys of pedigree fetch more in some markets. Or maybe I'll take your sweet sister and have my men do to her what they did with your pretty little girlfriend?"

To his credit, he doesn't flinch, though he does look like he's about to fall over.

He spits blood at her and grins. "You fucking bitch. You don't get it, do you? You're taking no one."

Then he stabs her in the neck with my dagger and passes the fuck out.

SEVENTEEN

LORCAN

THE BITCH IS DEAD.

And I'm going under. The drugs are clouding my head, chalking up my veins, pulling me into oblivion.

For a brief second, my eyes flicker open and I see fucking Aurora's ghost standing over, looking down on me. She's covered in blood, soulless as the day she died, the smile on her lips fucking terrifying.

"Now I have to clean up your fucking mess?" she says, cocking her head. The voice that comes out of her mouth isn't Aurora's, but I know it.

"Who the fuck are you?" I slur, though I already know who she is.

Tory.

Her piercing gaze bears down as my eyes falter and I drift off. But not before I hear her say, "Only your worst nightmare."

I claw myself awake, breathing hard like I've run a fucking marathon. My head pounds. My mouth tastes like fucking ash.

The sound of someone clearing their throat has me bolting upright. Or I would if I wasn't bound to a bed by my limbs, unable to move.

Ropes burn my wrists as I wrench against them, scanning the room. It's a bedroom, but it's not mine. Cheap, tarnished wallpaper hangs off the walls. Light spills through some yellow floral curtains, slicing into my eyeballs if I so much as look at it dead on. The place is airless, colder than a nun's cunt, and stinks of piss.

A beautiful vixen sits in the chair in the corner of the room, looking at me like she wants to kill me—if the knife on her lap is anything to go by, she does.

I regard her stoically, ignoring the spike of adrenaline flooding my veins, and then I see it. It's Tory, with long locks of pale blonde rather than the shitty brown it was before. Her eyes seem different too—colder, darker. Eyes I could drown in.

What the fuck is going on? Where am I?

Did we fuck last night or something? I can't fucking remember.

Maybe we did. I'm half-naked and so is she. She's in a black bra, black hot pants, and some stockings. She looks fucking glorious. Pert breasts popping out of her corseted bra, fishnets over long, pale legs, and exotic, almond-shaped eyes that a man can fall into and never come out of.

I hope we haven't fucked. The first time I sink between her soft thighs, I want to be wide awake when I shove my cock deep inside her and make her beg to take it in every way possible.

Fuck. I've got it bad. Saskia was right.

I'm obsessed.

With a sigh, I run my gaze over her perfect form once more, letting her see the desire in my eyes. She observes me back with an expression of absolute disgust, making my dick twitch.

"What's going on, sweetheart?" I say, tugging at the ropes around my forearms, hardly moving them an inch. The siren has me tied up good and tight.

"Good. You're awake. I was beginning to think you'd died on me," she says.

I raise my brows. "You were worried about me?"

"Not for the reason you think," she shoots back.

"Fair enough, sweetheart," I drawl. "Untie me and we'll call it even."

"No," she says, looking at me with sardonic eyes. "I like you tied up."

I snort a laugh. "Sas was right. You are a crazy fucking bitch."

Saskia warned me that this one was a bunny boiler. I didn't believe her until I saw her stalking me around campus a few times, following me home. I thought about kidnapping her a few times, just to see if she'd let me break her. Some girls dig the captive shit. Maybe I do. Maybe this is my Stephen King's *Misery* fucking moment happening right here, right now. *Why does that make me so damn hard?*

Her eyes flash with something dark. *Anger?* I watch her twiddle her blade in her hands. I remember sticking *that* blade in Blair's fucking throat. *The bitch had better be dead.*

I pull at my binds again and then study her from my position on the bed. "Tory," I say softly. "Untie me."

It's not a request.

She doesn't make a fucking move to do anything but feast her eyes on my body. Her lack of respect drives me fucking crazy. More hazy images of last night pound into my brain—finding Tory in my bedroom, shoving her down onto my bed, wanting to fuck her brains out for trespassing...

My cock tenses and my eyes become slits.

Tory takes all of me in and then comes over to where I'm spruced up like a fucking offering and straddles me. The sensation of her sliding over me, legs on either side, has my dick hard and my eyes wandering.

The corners of her lips tug into a smile. Of course, I'm going to be fucking turned on. I'm not dead and she's a goddamn goddess. Even more so with her long, ash-blonde hair that's ripe for wrapping around my fist.

"I hate it when a guy calls me crazy. It makes me want to do crazy things," she says as she gives a moan and rubs herself over me, gliding the flat edge of the blade over my chest.

Okay, I take it back.

I've no idea where the fuck I am, or why she has me tied up to torture me with her pussy, but I'm not about to complain. *Who'd have thought an angel would have such a dark side.*

"Maybe I like crazy," I say.

She tilts her head, big brown orbs no longer blue stealing the life out of mine. "Was Aurora crazy too?"

"Aurora?" *What the fuck is she talking about now?*

"Is that why you killed her?" The edge of her knife is pressed against my side, the angle of it cutting in.

I narrow my eyes. "You think I had something to do with..." My words trail off as she tugs Aurora's diary, the one I had stashed in my bedroom desk drawer, out from the back pocket of her shorts and drops it onto my chest. The bound journal is cold against my skin.

Tory leans forward until our faces are so close that I can smell her sweet breath, and she teases the point of her dagger right on my jugular. "I know you did."

I shrug, or as much as you can trussed up the way I am with a fucking dagger rammed up against my neck. "That girl was delusional. I wouldn't believe any-*fucking*-thing she wrote in there if I were you."

She looks at me, eyes dark and curious. "So, you two weren't dating?"

"We were fucking. That's all." The corner of my mouth twitches into a smirk. "Didn't know you cared, sweetheart."

"Oh, I don't. I'm more interested in why you have her diary in the first place, and the blood-stained lock of her hair you kept with it."

Eyes smoldering, holding steel under my chin, she looks fucking glorious. I would love nothing more than to have her tight, little psycho-ass tied up beneath me. I wouldn't waste time. I'd bury my cock so balls deep inside her, she'd scream my name for days. *I should have kidnapped her first. I'd have enjoyed this a hell of a lot more.*

"You want the truth?" I ask her.

"That would be helpful."

"She asked for it."

She frowns, digging the point of the blade in enough to draw blood. "You admit it? You killed her?"

"Not in the way you think," I say.

"What do you mean?"

"If you've read her diary then you already know," I say, keeping my gaze guarded.

She looks at me with equally unreadable eyes. "I want to hear it from you."

"We don't all get what we want."

Her brown eyes harden. She grabs the front of my boxers, using the edge of the knife to cut the material away until I'm fully erect in front of her. All I can do is lie there and watch her. It's kinky as fuck. Especially when she takes my thick shaft in her icy hands and plays with me until I'm raging hard and ready.

Suddenly, she slips and pain erupts over the length of my dick. The bitch slashed me with her nails. I suck air between my teeth and shoot her a dark look.

"I can do this all night, *sweetheart*," she says, her lips turning up at the edges into a mocking, unnatural smile.

Fucking bitch.

"Fine," I say, my tone bored. "She begged me to do it. Is that what you want to hear?"

"Why was she hung up from the common room ceiling?"

"You don't want to know," I say darkly. I also can't talk about it while she's holding my cock. There are some parts of fucking ugly you just don't go to willingly.

"Oh, I do. I really do." She gives my cock a hard yank, making my eyes water. "*Tell* me."

I grimace at her. *Psycho Bunny is going to pay for that.*

"Look, no one gets out, not unless they're dead. They fucking own us, Aurora couldn't handle it. When she turned up at my house in the middle of the night, pathetic and half beaten to death and asked me to end it, I was fucking happy to. They found out and took care of the rest."

My jaw is clenched after my outburst, so I force it to relax. I gave Tory the fucking PG version. If she wants more than that, she's not getting it from me.

She looks confused. Her mouth opens to speak but I get there first. I'm done with talking about this shit. Either we fuck, or she does whatever crazy shit she dragged me here to do. I couldn't care less. Whoever she is, whoever she's working for, I don't give a fuck anymore.

I was dead the moment I killed Blair.

"Are we gonna fuck now?" I say in a lazy tone. I'm not going to say fucking no. It may be my last ever chance. And she's gorgeous, even if she is a few screws loose. Aurora was a little unstable too. *Maybe crazy's my type?*

The smirk is on my lips before I can stop it.

"What's so amusing, Duke?" Tory snaps.

I look up at her through half-lidded eyes. "You're the fucking Devil, but I still want you."

She stares back, before moving her hips, grinding herself onto me. I shut my eyes, enjoying the sensation until a sharper pain penetrates my side. I drag my eyes open and glance at the blade in her hands, just in time to see a thin line of blood trailing behind it.

"Do you still want me now?" she asks sweetly.

"Even more," I hiss as she pulls the edge all the way down, watching my reaction with doleful eyes. And then draws the blade over my stomach to my groin, giving me a sick, twisted little smile.

My goddamn dick is throbbing, but I tense as she grips the full length of me in her fist.

"Are you scared I'll cut it off?" she asks, her tone playful and light.

"Nah, I'm just really turned the fuck on."

This answer seems to satisfy her because she starts jacking me off again. As soon as I'm solid in her hands, she shrugs out of her shorts. My hungry eyes consume every part of her pretty, pink, shaved little pussy.

What fucking torture.

"Don't come inside of me, or I'll fucking stab you," she says and slides herself down over my rigid cock.

Actual fucking torture. Kill me now.

Then she fucks me, touching herself as she does, holding the cold blade to my neck like she might just slice me from ear to ear if I shoot my load inside of her. So fucking wet and tight, the sweet feeling of Tory gliding up and down over my dick makes me groan out loud and my eyes roll back in my head.

I need to cum. It's tempting, and I'm so fucking close. She's panting hard, and so am I. *These fucking restraints.* If they weren't holding me down…

I jerk against them, gritting my teeth as the knife's edge tears into me. But I don't fucking care. The look in her eyes is pure desire mixed with something darker. It's a look I know too well….

I let her see just how much I want to do this to her, and then some.

Because if she ever lets me out of these bonds…I absolutely fucking will.

You can count on that.

EIGHTEEN

VIOLA

FUCKING ISN'T *part of the plan, Viola.*

But now I have him where I want him, in Dante's cabin, I can't help but taste him a little. It's been a very long time since a guy turned me on to the point I can't resist. There's something about the way he looks at me. And now I don't have to fucking pretend anymore…

I want him.

It's his eyes. They tell me he doesn't give a fuck if he lives or dies.

And I have a thing for pretty, huge cocks.

He's hard for me the moment I lower myself onto him, the tip of his cock hot and teasing at my entrance. Then I push down, and he fills me beautifully.

His starving eyes, soulless like mine, are watching as I fuck him slowly. He grunts beneath me, pulling against his restraints. I love that he can't move. That it's my blade pressed against his throat while I get myself off.

He wants to be free. He wants to control me. But he can't.

I grind onto him over and over until we're both slick with

sweat. Eventually, the void inside me fills with a rawness that's completely and utterly different from taking a life. Then, I lean forward and kiss him hard. His tongue dives inside, teeth tearing at my lips, sucking my breath away until it's my blood I'm tasting.

It sends me over the edge.

Waves of intense pleasure ripple from my core as I moan out loud. Beneath me, panting hard, I feel him begin to peak. *No.* I snatch a handful of his hair and shove the tip of my dagger into the flesh of his shoulder, soaking us both in the warmth of his blood.

He grits his teeth, orbs blazing with fury as he strains against his bonds. I look into his clear, green eyes as my orgasm shudders through me.

"Don't you dare come," I say softly with a dangerous edge to my voice. "Or I'll do more than cut your dick off."

I close my eyes and arch my back, riding the last of it, enjoying the release of fucking ecstasy. Then I ease myself off as he groans, leaving the blade partly buried in his shoulder.

There's blood everywhere. His body is slick with it. And he's still absolutely rock hard. I trace a bloody finger down his abs all the way to the head of his cock, loving the way it throbs under my touch.

"You're just going to leave me like this?" he rasps, eyes dark and wild.

"You're lucky I took you this far."

If I was being nice, I'd finish him off, but I'm in a shitty mood. And I don't do nice. There's no advantage to being nice.

None whatsoever.

His eyes are unfocused and full of frustration as I reach into the bedside drawer and take out a vial of drugs and a fresh needle.

"Use me and abuse me, huh?" he says thickly.

"At least you're not dead yet," I counter and stick the needle into the nearest raised vein on his arm. Almost instantly, his eyes flutter closed, and he crashes into a deep, dark sleep.

I clean and dress the superficial wounds on Lorcan's body, and then shower and change. When I come out of the bathroom, I'm in no mood for games. I have several missed calls from Polina and Dante, and a few messages from Dino.

I ring only Dante back.

After the stunt Lorcan pulled, turning his bedroom into a fucking crime scene, I had to move fast. I dragged the body into the hidden doorway, closed it over, and called Dante to come over and help me clean up. Then, I retrieved my knife, coaxed a drugged-up Lorcan downstairs and into my car, and drove him here. The house party was in full swing at that time, so no one paid us any attention as we left.

I did have time to read Aurora's diary while waiting for him to wake up. It corroborates his story somewhat. Aurora documented everything in it that happened to her, right up until the point she went to Lorcan for help.

He wasn't lying.

He killed her because she asked him to.

I'm not sure what to do with that. He might not be the type of target I enjoy killing, but he's still my target. Let's not add to the fact that I just used him as a human dildo. As nice as that was, I have a job to finish. Polina wouldn't be fucking happy if I didn't, considering that she's already paid me. And when have I not killed a target just because he was innocent?

Never.

Still, every time I think about killing him, there's an unnerving feeling lingering in the pit of my stomach from not knowing the end of the story. Like I'm shutting the pages of a book halfway through the middle, burning the only copy until all that's left is ash.

It leaves a shitty taste in my mouth.

But one I can live with.

Maybe I'll kill him. Maybe I won't.

I haven't decided yet.

"You're in trouble," Dante says as soon as he answers.

"No shit. Did you get rid of it?"

"The place is like new. I had to take out the men searching for your boy, and then wait for everyone to leave to dispose of the bodies. You owe me, V."

"Bill me for it," I say with a sigh.

"Give me half the fee for killing the target, and we'll call it even."

"About that."

"You haven't done it yet, have you?"

"Define 'done'."

Dante sighs down the line. "V. She's going to crucify you. Where are you? Are you at my cabin?"

"Stall her for me. I need more time. He's injured. If I do it now, it won't be clean." The lie is ash on my tongue.

"Fine. But you're running out of time."

Dante hangs up, and my phone rings immediately as I head back to the bedroom where Lorcan is. I glance down at the screen. It's Polina. I ignore it, jamming the device into my pocket, calmly viewing the sight of an empty bed amongst the bloody sheets that greets me as soon as I walk inside the room. The sound of my car roaring out of the farmhouse driveway confirms it.

Fuck.

I left him untied since he was out for the count while I saw to the gash on his shoulder.

Rookie *fucking* mistake.

Because Lorcan Duke is long gone.

Dante finally comes good with a replacement car. I reluctantly gave him the address so he could drop it off. So the weekend is spent watching Lorcan's house, although I never see him leave or enter so I don't even know if he's in the building or not. He might not be since my car is missing. It's not on the driveway. I consider going up, knocking on the door, and asking for it back, but when I see him again, I'd rather it be on neutral ground.

Like school.

On Monday, I'm relieved to see my Beetle parked in one of the student parking spaces at Sacred Heart. School feels pretty much the same as last week. Except that Lorcan is stalking me just as much as I'm stalking him.

All day he's been making eyes at me, and all fucking day I've been ignoring him. The only solace is seeing his arm in a sling and a burning hunger in his eyes whenever he looks my way. Fucking him was probably the best thing I could have done, apart from killing him, because now he has a taste, I can guarantee he'll want more.

Polina hasn't stopped pestering me either. The longer I don't answer, the more likely it is that I won't kill him the way she wants. Or even the way *I* want. A bullet to the brain, while he's getting his morning coffee, is cleaner and smarter.

But it's also goddamn boring.

And I don't do fucking guns.

I skip double Italian because I despise languages after a lifetime of moving around, country to country. I'm fluent in all the necessary ones. Italian is a pretty language but it's also worthless to me, given that my father's side of the family has disowned me.

I also can't be fucked to pretend to go to class right now. I need to study Aurora's diary. I specifically want to know who hurt her so badly that she wanted to take her own life.

If it wasn't Lorcan, who was it?

The darkness in me has been rising. I can feel it whenever someone cuts me up in traffic, pushes me in the corridor, or serves me the wrong food order.

I'm. On. Edge.

There's a risk I'll snap soon, and if I don't have a chosen outlet, I'll destroy someone who doesn't deserve it. Not that I give a fuck about who I end up killing. I just don't want to get caught. Over the years, I've found one thing to be true—no one comes looking to seek justice for the monsters. And the darker they are, the more depraved I get to be.

Stalking Lorcan, screwing him, cutting him up—hasn't quenched my thirst.

It's only made me crave another release.

NINETEEN

AURORA

13th September

Dear Diary,
    Don't let them smell fresh blood.

Those are the words Jude whispered in my ear this morning, as I left the house for my first day back at Sacred Heart.

I got as far as the front door before he called my name. He strode right up to me in the hallway and took hold of my wrist. He held it so hard I know it's going to leave a bruise. He smelled of cigarettes and booze, and his eyes were ringed-red. He looked broken. His words of wisdom actually hurt my ear before he vanished back into the depths of the house.

I hate that house. I hate my cousin. I hate them all.

Because that's not usually how it goes. My suave and sophisticated older cousin doesn't *usually* give me a second glance when I'm at home. He certainly doesn't find me before school to give me advice. He's popular. Too busy with girls and playing rugby.

Why does he see me now?

I stood there like an idiot waiting for some sort of explanation. A million thoughts whirling through my mind. *Should I chase him down? Ask him what the bloody hell he's playing at?*

The grandfather clock snapped me out of it. Then I left that house so fast, taking the steps of the front porch two at a time, sliding into the waiting car without so much as a backward glance. I usually drive myself into school, but no one wants me behind the wheel after what happened.

I'm also not sure I'm capable of driving.

After Jude's words, all I wanted to do was rest my head against the cold glass of the window and stare out at the blossom trees lining the boulevards as we drove past.

I hate the village too, with its tightly-packed charming cottages. Every house is the same. Every avenue is identical. Maybe that gate or a certain bush is shaped a little differently, or there's a splash of color here and there, but otherwise every row is pretty much a carbon copy of the last. Until you get to the expensive streets like ours.

It's such a hideous village—Whitechapel. I don't know why we moved here. And I don't know why this bothers me now. It never used to. It could be that the last few days have been strange. Even this feels off—Jude staying at home while I go into Sacred Heart alone. It's all wrong. I'm not the eldest, Cece is. She's not even here. I've no idea why our parents want him at home, and Cece abroad, today of all days. It can't be a coincidence that I'm starting my senior year just when he's taking leave. That I'm going in alone just when the sharks are circling.

Something is up.

I just don't know what.

His words keep echoing through my mind. *Don't let them smell fresh blood.* He means the other students. My older, more popular cousin, who doesn't usually notice that I even exist, is trying to warn me. *Why?* Most of the time he acts like we're not even related. I'm the youngest of the Marques family. The last one to attend the prestigious Sacré-Cœur. The last one to leave the sanctity of our home without a bodyguard following me day and night. The last one to do anything.

The radio annoyed me too this morning. The driver has it set to classical music just as my mother likes, with the occasional interruption from traffic or news alerts.

That's how I heard there was another murder in the outskirts of the city. There's always murder happening here. We're not supposed to talk about dead bodies or any negative things in the house. It's bad karma. And you never know who's listening in. Though, it wasn't hard to overhear my parents after they'd had a few bottles of wine.

Murder made to look like an accident. That's what Daddy said. It makes me wonder if that's what they think happened to B…

Fuck, B, why did you leave me here? All I do is wait for the pain to subside and grow numb like it does after a while. Because no one cares. They even had another baby so they could forget it ever happened.

I can't.

I'm supposed to, though. I'm supposed to pretend I know absolutely nothing even though I know more about how life works from attending Sacred Heart than any life lessons my parents could teach me. That place is a nest of devil spawn and the adults have no fucking clue. Everyone thinks the school, the students, and the teachers are perfect.

It's not. It's hell.

When I finally got to school, the courtyard was empty except for me and the driver. I'm not supposed to be back today, so all the students and teachers were still at morning assembly.

My parents told everyone I was attending art school this summer in Germany. I sort of was until last night when my mother called and demanded I return home. *Step up to the mark, Aurora. Do your part, Aurora. Don't cause a fuss, Aurora.*

Two hours later, I was on a charter home. Six hours later, I was packed and ready for Sacred Heart. *To come back.* I never wanted or expected to come back to this place. I thought I'd gotten out.

You didn't get very far, did you, Aurora? You got as far as Berlin before the dogs were set loose and they dragged you back. Good job on getting out. Good job on getting sucked down into the middle of this hell hole all over again.

I was going to ask permission to stay in Berlin. It felt *safe* there. Even if they did take my phone away from me. Even if I wasn't allowed sharp objects like paintbrushes and pencils for all the pretty pictures they encouraged me to make. It didn't bother me to only use my fingers and hands. There's something to be said for smearing it raw and dripping onto a blank canvas. My therapist was intrigued why I preferred it that way. My mother was shocked.

I just liked the way it looked on my hands.

And I was making progress…

But now I'm back in the place where it feels like a hundred pairs of invisible eyes are watching me, making me aware of my own vulnerability. I feel sick inside just thinking about it. I can't quite breathe.

All I have to do is survive.

After the bell rang the halls started to overflow with students. Those invisible eyes felt no longer unseen. All of them looked at me. Some dipped their heads to whisper but most snickered behind their hands, saying cruel words out loud so everyone could hear. This is why I didn't want to come back. Not to this school. Not to these students.

Not after what I did.

She couldn't handle it. She went off the rails.

She's fucking insane.

Did you hear where her parents sent her? She's been in a looney bin this entire fucking time.

I shrunk myself down, trying to disappear. Somehow, I found my locker and got the books I needed. I left my therapy journal and a romance paperback I stole from my mother's library in the locker. I probably shouldn't have brought my diary of secrets with me. However, it's important that I keep up with my art and that I have an outlet for expression.

Not having one is the whole reason I got into this mess in the first place, according to my therapist. I severely doubt that having a blank page to draw on makes you any less crazy but there was no way I was going to leave it at home. We have an open door policy now and Mother is on the rampage since I got back. I have no desire to share my secrets with her.

She would kill me herself if she knew what I did to survive here. She would also slaughter me if she knew I'd taken a book from her special top shelf. Of that, there's no question.

Someone brushed past me, I didn't see who, shoving my shoulder so I hit the locker, dropping all of my books. They laughed all around me when they saw that.

As I bent down to pick up my strewn books, resisting the urge to rub the new ache in my shoulder, I heard his voice.

And just like that everything wasn't so bad.

If I could *want* anything. If I *needed* anyone. If I *missed* one person....

It would be him.

Lorcan Duke.

Tingles ran up and down my arms when I heard him. My body remembered. I didn't even need to look and my heart was pounding all over, my mouth already bone dry.

I wanted to forget he attended here.

Liar.

Blood rushed in my ears. The sound of everyone around me fell away until only his voice mattered.

I'd love more than anything to spin around right now and see him striding down the halls to me as I take him in.

My eyes have been hungry for him, starved.

It took everything to concentrate on closing my locker properly. I knew it wasn't me he was approaching, but I wanted to pretend that it was. That the dream was real, and he was still mine.

I knew I should have just gone to class, but my body refused to move. I heard him and his boys laughing, bringing all my buried emotions flooding to the surface. A prickle of dread clutched my stomach. I wanted to run away. I wanted to run to him.

I wanted to die.

My eyes are now drawn to my wrists where the scars are. Apparently, I didn't cut right. I cut the wrong way so I didn't die fast enough. Jude found me.

Fucking Jude.

Anyway, Diary, I digress. I did find the courage to glance at him just once, letting my eyes dart over to him for what felt like an age but was merely only a second or two. Until my breath caught and the dull ache in my chest threatened to choke me.

And then, I forced myself to turn around and walk away.

Away from Lorcan Duke.

Who knew my childhood crush would be just as debilitating and just as crippling in my senior year as in my junior one. And that it still hurts… so badly.

Lorcan, still polished and as beautiful as he ever was, somehow ended up behind me.

Boys—they walk so fast. Long legs I suppose. From what I could make out, Lorcan was talking to Finn Baron as they walked to class. Lorcan's charming accent still gives me butterflies just to hear it.

As he came alongside, I allowed myself a tiny glance. He was wearing the boys' version of the Sacred Heart uniform. But boys in schools don't usually look as mature or confident as him. He gives off an unshakable air like he owns this school and everyone in it. Like he's a god.

Of course he does. He's a goddamn Duke.

And I'm a Marques. I must not forget that.

That thought does little for my own nerves. Even though the

Dukes have always acted superior to my family in every way, there was a time when being a Marques meant something. Not anymore. Not since my father made a mistake and the family has been paying the price to the Dukes ever since. Not since B died and I just lost it.

Lorcan never looked at me like I was anything more than an itch to scratch.

I've no idea if he even cares that I still exist. And even if he does, he probably sees me like everyone else now.

Like I'm fucked in the head.

So I just kept my focus on walking. One step in front of the other. Lorcan and Finn were so deep in discussion and I was able to catch snatches of what they were saying as they prowled past. I lowered my chin, keeping my eyes glued to the floor, unable to look at anything other than the parquet flooring before me, and the toes of my shoes as they treaded quietly.

They were walking so fast that I ended up matching their pace and tilting my head, to sneak another eyeful of my old flame.

At that same moment, Lorcan looked up and our eyes met. They widened, cold recognition flaring for the briefest second in his mesmerizing green orbs, before he locked his emotions down. And like that, I couldn't breathe.

From under the messy, dark bangs that fell over his face, Lorcan's gaze continued to look my way, startling me into openly staring back. He still has that disarming smile he had back in second grade. The smile that caught my attention and made me want to kiss him.

I wish I could kiss him now.

Never once has he ever said a bad word to me or tried to hurt me. Even if he forgot me, he's never been like the others. He is the best of Sacred Heart. He's not meant to have a malicious bone in his body.

All I could give him was a weak smile and then I quickly averted my eyes, wishing I could close them. *Wishing I was miles away.*

Then I couldn't take it anymore. I pretended he wasn't there and carried on walking, staring straight ahead. Until I saw an exit and dashed for it.

Bleeding heart aside, it's for the best.

I don't know if they were still watching me, but I took my cute heels and stalked through the vestibule until I was no longer inside the interior of the school but outside of it.

My solitude was short-lived, however.

Through an open window someone threw an egg. I jumped back and it landed at my feet. Another hit me square in the chest, smearing into a gooey mess on impact.

"Have you got egg on your face now you're back, Aurora?" someone shouted through the open window. There was a volley of laughter after it.

I wanted the door to hell to open beneath my feet and demons to drag me away from all this. But all I did was wipe the stain as best I could and make my way to registration.

I remember now. It wasn't B dying that sent me over the edge.

It was Lorcan forgetting who I was.

TWENTY

VIOLA

TUESDAY, I skip school. Go for my usual early morning run to help clear my head. Then I drive to Quinn's place.

Her office is a technological haven in the middle of a backroad industrial estate. I park where she can see me, and wave at the camera at the entrance. It doesn't take long for her to buzz me in, retracting the steel bars that barricade the door.

Quinn is ever so slightly paranoid about being caught and having her kneecaps and elbows shot out, and her face smashed in with a baseball bat. She supplies Polina with a lot of dirt, most of it on some very bad people. I can't say I blame her.

I'm one of those people.

Quinn hit on me in a nightclub bathroom once and I showed her a good time. She showed me how to erase all traces of my digital existence and invent new ones. I didn't know Quinn worked for Polina until she had all kinds of shit on me, and it was obvious she'd been paid to do it.

I eventually forgave her, since she never handed Polina the file and, of course, I promised to gut her if she did. She still comes over on weekends.

Or I go over to hers, like today.

Dark hair snatched back into a ponytail, glasses perched on the edge of her nose, Quinn looks up as I enter. She's in her gym gear, making herself a smoothie in her office kitchen. She pours some of the green looking sludge into an extra glass and hands it to me.

I take a sip and immediately ditch it on the counter, making a face.

"Hey, that's kale and cucumber." She frowns.

"Tastes like snot. Do you have any orange juice?

She juts her chin in the direction over her shoulder. "In the fridge."

I help myself and wander over to where Quinn is waiting for me at a workstation of computers set up in the middle of the room. I grab a seat next to her.

"You're here for the surveillance tapes, right?"

"You managed to get all of them?"

She lifts a perfect brow. "Do you even know me?"

"You're not infallible," I say.

She half-smirks but it fades quickly as she taps quickly on her keyboard. "It was tough, but I hacked in and erased every trace of you at that club. These are local copies of the main highlights. I haven't wiped them yet. I thought you might want to see this before I do."

"You couldn't share it on the drive?"

"The agency still has access. They would have removed it immediately."

I give her a curious look. "Why would the agency do that?"

"You'll see."

I take a sip of my OJ and motion Quinn to play.

"There's no audio, but you can gather what's being said," she adds as the video starts. It's Lorcan entering the room. We watch for several minutes in silence. I see myself enter and then leave, and then….

Quinn gets up. "I've seen it. I don't need to see it again." She walks off to the other side of her office, leaving me to watch it all the way to the end. After it's done, she comes back.

"I'm going to delete it, but I wanted you to see it."

I give Quinn a long hard stare. "Why?'

"Because…" she starts and then stops, voice breaking.

"Because of what I do?"

She nods, eyes glistening.

"He's a killer," I say.

She scoffs, wiping beneath her eyes. "And you fucking wonder why."

After the videos are deleted and I've got what I came for, Quinn gives me a hug. She's probably the only person I'll let so close without needing permission.

She hugs me tight and nestles her face into the crook of my neck. "Why don't you stay the night," she murmurs. "I've got a bottle of wine in the fridge."

Fuck knows I could use the release, but as much as I want to stay, I'm also itching to go. I shake my head and untangle myself from Quinn's arms. I give her a peck on the cheek because it's the right thing to do, and then step back.

"I can't. I have school tomorrow. I need to get going."

She smiles and nods. "There's someone else, isn't there?"

Quinn and I were never exclusive, but she knows me well enough to figure out when my attention is elsewhere. I don't know what to say to that, so I say nothing.

It's only as she watches me drive away that I realize she's wrong.

It's not someone else.

It's several someones….

I'm fucked, because I'm meant to be killing at least one of them.

I didn't call Polina back, so the next day the only message from her is three words an assassin for hire never wants to see…

You're fucking fired.

Less than an hour later, my replacement shows up at Sacred Heart. The technical support van in the parking lot is so glaringly obvious that I call Dante the moment I see it.

"She sent Pierre? I'm insulted."

"V, don't be. He's cheap and she's desperate. And you're making her look bad. Do you blame her?"

"Is he here for me too? Because it's a fucking joke if he is."

"She's underestimating you."

"Damn right she is." I hang up.

Stalking my own killer doesn't take long. I find Pierre fiddling underneath Lorcan's car in the boathouse car park. There are no cameras this far from campus, hence why the students prefer to hang out here. So it's simple enough to stab him in the leg with one of his screwdrivers, wait for him to yell at me and try to scramble out from under the car, and then drive another one through his left eye socket and into his brain.

I check the car to make sure it's not going to blow up my boy or disfigure him in a car crash, and then I drag the body into the van and drive it to Dante's cabin.

Walking home takes me a couple of hours, but it's worth it to not have to dispose of it myself.

If I knew where Polina lived I'd leave it at her house, but I don't have that information. Quinn has it but she won't tell me. And it's probably a bad idea anyhow. Even so, if I knew where Polina fucking lived, I'd dump the body in her driveway in a heartbeat.

Scrap that. I'd probably kill her. Quinn is really the only person keeping that bitch alive right now.

It's late evening by the time I get to my apartment, take a shower, and change. Falling into bed, I make up my mind that I'm not going to kill Lorcan now purely on principle.

I don't like to be rushed.

And I certainly don't like to be replaced.

Ever.

I spend the rest of the day making sure no other hits are made, and doing the exact opposite of what the agency hired me to do—protecting Lorcan. I'm a better killer than I am a bodyguard but needs must.

After classes, I locate Cecilia Marques in the boathouse. She tenses when she sees me but doesn't make a move to leave.

I make hostile eyes at the girls she's with. "Leave."

They sweep their gazes over me but don't make a move to do as I ask.

I glance at Cecilia in askance. She draws in a breath and then gives them a reluctant nod. At her command, they scatter out of the boathouse and onto the deck where most of the students are lounging on the outdoor seating, drinking alcohol, smoking drugs, and listening to music.

Lorcan is among them beside Saskia, with his entourage surrounding them both like they're the king and queen of Sacred Heart. Her head is on his shoulder.

Lorcan stops talking and looks up at me, and everyone stares my way as my presence is made known. Lorcan's green eyes darken into pools of desire. He takes a swig of his beer and smirks.

"Missed you in class yesterday, sweetheart. I hope you're not avoiding me."

"I wouldn't dream of it," I say.

"This is a private party. Why don't you fuck off back where you came from?" Saskia's voice is full of sharp edges. It makes me think of razor blades down a chalkboard.

"Leave it, Sas." Lorcan rolls his eyes. "She can stay."

Of course, I'm fucking staying.

I take the seat next to Cecilia and place Aurora's diary discreetly between us.

Her brow creases as she sees it, then she lets out a lungful of air. "I fucking knew it. My father hired you to kill Lor, didn't he?"

"What makes you say that?"

She sighs, deeper this time. "My father hires everyone to do the things he can't. It's what he does. He's so trapped by family loyalty bullshit that he can't do anything for himself. Well, he has it wrong, it wasn't Lorcan who hurt Aurora. Lorcan saved her, but fucking Daddy won't listen to me." She takes a mouthful of her drink. "He never has."

"You know who it is behind all this, though, don't you?"

She gnaws her bottom lip.

"What's going on, Cecilia? Tell me. Why was a fucking teacher about to rape you at the club?"

"It's bigger than him, than just one person," she says, shaking her head.

"Then tell me who is at the top."

She closes her eyes. "I can't."

"Who are you protecting?"

She sighs, refocusing on me. "Everyone here. We're all fucking involved."

I quirk a brow. "You're going to have to explain a little better than that."

She takes another drink and then stares at the bottle in her hands, picking at the label. I wait while she gets comfortable. I've found that people who let their emotions rule them need me to do that sometimes, even if I don't understand why.

"It started when we were kids. As we got older, we recruited more kids until the bastards had an entire network. The more you recruit the less they focus on you. So at first, we wanted to bring others. It was only later we decided to protect the younger ones by offering ourselves. It was Lorcan's idea. Some couldn't handle it, like my sister, but most of us do what's necessary. We just pretend it's not happening. Others, Lorcan mainly, wants to make them pay one day," she says with a bitter snort. "Like that would ever happen."

Everything she said makes sense. The burning need that has

forever been lurking in the pit of my heart, ignites into a hot flame. I'm not upset about these kids. Shit happens. I'm annoyed that my hunger is clawing away at my insides and there's a ripe peach of evil I haven't sunk my teeth into yet. And I'm frustrated that I have to fucking wait.

Gripping my dagger hilt over the material of my pleated wool skirt, I breathe deeply, brushing aside the way it makes my skin crawl.

Not yet my love, not yet.

I force the darkness back and glance at the pathetic girl in front of me who can't bring herself to look into my eyes. It's just as well, I'm not good at hiding what I am sometimes.

"You're not going to tell me who *they* are, are you?" I say, uncurling my hand from the dagger to pick up Aurora's diary.

Her gaze flicks to the diary, to me, and then over to Lorcan. She gets to her feet, giving me a weak smile that doesn't reach her eyes.

"Did you know that Lorcan and Saskia are adopted? The Dukes can't have children. I think there's a reason God took away Joseph Duke's ability to reproduce, if you know what I mean," she says, placing her empty beer bottle stripped of its label on the table next to me and then disappears outside.

As Cecilia walks away, I get up to leave, tapping out a message to Quinn to dig into the adoption. I want her to send me everything she can find on Joseph Duke and his reasons for being childless.

In the outer hallway, where the boats are stacked near the exit to the car park, I hear a smooth baritone voice.

"Looking for another fuckboy to tie up and torture?"

I glance up from my phone and into the regal gaze of Lorcan Duke blocking my exit.

"Oh, it's you."

He steps forward until he's almost right on top of me, his citrusy and woody scent reminding me of the night when he was my fuck doll, and I could do with him what I wanted.

"Come with me, Tory. If that's even your name," he says, walking past me out of the boathouse.

I follow him outside. The lake is a black mirror reflecting the moon as we walk past it to where the cars are parked. There's a sleek-looking vehicle with tinted windows waiting. He opens the door and gestures for me to enter. I slip into the backseat facing him, hyper-aware of the car doors locking as soon as they close. I'm not worried. If he tried anything I have a needle full of drugs prepped in my blazer pocket, not to mention my dagger nestled in its usual place.

"It's not your name, is it?" Lorcan asks as soon as the doors are closed. When I don't reply, he answers for me.

"Carl Marques sent you after me because of what I did to his daughter, Aurora. Isn't that right, Viola?" he says, throwing a file in my lap. I open it. It's my employee file from the agency database. No one should be able to get hold of this.

No one.

"Where did you get this?"

"Viola Hawkes. Twenty-three years old. Fluent in over twenty different languages. In-depth pharmaceutical knowledge. Knife skills…" he starts reciting the front page out loud and off by heart.

"Where did you fucking get this?" I repeat.

His eyes blaze with the same intensity as the other night. "Where's Blair's fucking body?"

"Is Blair the one you made a hash job of murdering?"

"Dead is fucking dead. Just tell me where the body is."

"I had a friend deal with it," I say cryptically. "Why?"

He breathes out sharply. "There was a black notebook that Blair kept in her right breast pocket. I need it."

"Well, I don't have it."

"I don't think you understand. I don't take no for an answer, sweetheart."

"Neither do I," I say.

He looks at me blankly for a few seconds and then scoffs.

I shift to get a better angle. If this gets ugly, I want to be closer to his injured arm.

"Cecilia told me what the deal is here," I say carefully, filling the short silence.

"Oh, brilliant. What did she say?"

"That London's most powerful crime family runs some sort of sick child prostitution ring at Sacred Heart."

The muscle in his jaw ticks.

"She also said that you're adopted."

"Cecilia talks too much," he retorts, his clear green eyes looking away as his fingers dig into the soft leather of his armrest.

I continue. "Why does Carl Marques want you dead?"

Lorcan shrugs, eyes flitting back to meet mine. "I'm a threat. After he married Tatiana, my aunt, he assumed old Grandaddy Duke was going to leave everything to his one and only grandson, their son."

I think back to the files Quinn sent me. Byron. That was his name. "I thought their son committed suicide."

"He did. They had another one soon after."

"Let me guess, as soon as Joseph Duke and his wife, Katia, adopted you and Saskia it all changed?"

"I get on with Grandfather. He always wanted a grandson he could play chess and shoot rifles with. I was brought up to do both those things very well. Grandfather would have been dead by the time the Marques brat is old enough to apply for a hunting license."

"What about Aurora and Cecilia? Aren't they old enough?"

Lorcan's eyes darken. "They're female. He doesn't give a fuck about his daughters. He sold them both to Blair the first chance he got."

"Your family's actually more fucked up than mine," I say honestly.

He gives a harsh laugh. "Says the psycho bitch who almost sliced off my rotor cuff."

I cock my head at him. "You weren't complaining the other night."

He looks me up and down, eyes filling with desire, and then leans forward in his seat. I tense up, ready for whatever he can throw at me. Smirking like he wanted to see my reaction, he pauses.

I glare, shaking my head.

That's when he lunges.

His hands are all over my body, tearing at my clothes. He tastes of liquor as his tongue sweeps inside my mouth, biting, bruising, devouring me. I assault him back for a few brief seconds, hungry for him ever since that night in the cabin.

"Viola Hawkes," he hisses in my ear as he pushes me down on the backseat, trapping me underneath him. "I'm going to fucking enjoy breaking you apart."

My breath hitches, and my heart fucking races like it's going to explode. I grab his wounded shoulder and dig my fingers in, making him roar with pain.

"Fucking bitch," he says hoarsely, eyes feral, frantically pulling back. "Are you trying to kill me?"

"Don't do that again," I say, easing myself out from under him.

Eyes insidious, he snarls. "You're fucking crazy."

That's it.

My other hand is already in my blazer pocket curled around the needle in there. I whip it out and jab him in the thigh, making him yell like a dying fucking bear. He's lucky I didn't plunge the contents of the thing into his leg, because he'd be going into cardiac arrest right now if I did. I yank it out and slide back, breathing hard, waiting.

His eyes are dark, swirling fiery pits of rage.

The look suits him.

For a few heartbeats, we sit either side of the back seat, drawing in breaths, glaring at one another.

The blacked-out partition between the driver and the rear seats slowly comes down. A concerned-looking, heavy-set man eyes us from the front driver seat. "Everything alright, sir?" he says to Duke.

"Fucking fine," says Lorcan.

We stare at each other for a few seconds longer while the partition rises back up.

"Viola, I need that notebook," says Lorcan finally, a dark scowl marring his pretty face.

"I told you, I don't have it."

He glances at the file and its contents scattered on the floor. "It would be a shame if any of that found its way into the public domain."

"Are you threatening me? Because I could kill you now and not lose a fucking second of sleep over it."

He smirks. "Don't lie. You'd cry your fucking eyes out."

I smile back. "Don't underestimate me, love."

"Don't worry, sweetheart. I'm not."

There's the sound of a gun cocking. Lorcan's hand is hidden within the folds of his long overcoat but it's obvious he's pointing something right at me. "You have twenty-four hours to get the notebook, or I'm coming for you."

I tilt my head. "Cumming isn't your forte though, is it?"

He grins. "Next time, it'll be me on top and you tied to *my* bed. And I'll cum in whatever hole I fucking please."

There's the sound of the car unlocking, so I swing open the door and get out. I look him dead in the eyes before slamming the door in his face. "I'd like to see you fucking try."

I storm back to my car as his vehicle rolls away. I'm livid. Fucking raging. After I killed Pierre for him, how dare the fuckboy threaten me.

I'm going to kill him.

I'm going to destroy him.

But maybe after I fuck him senseless first because, after that little encounter, I'm horny as goddamn hell.

TWENTY-ONE

AURORA

21st September

Dear Diary,

Lorcan is such a pretty name.

I scrawled it several times in cursive letters across the center pages of my journal at lunchtime. I also watched my crush be the center of attention within his usual group of wankers and back stabbing bitches. Lorcan is so nice—I've no idea why he's friends with any of them. My sister Cecilia is back from her week away with her friends. She's ignoring me. Pretending I don't exist.

It doesn't matter. The common room was unusually crowded today, so I sat in the corner pretending to be engrossed in my writing because what else can I do. When I wasn't crazy, I used to hang out with them. Or sometimes I'd read in the far side corner, next to the silent study room. There was a lonely seat beside a thin bookshelf that I'd curl up on, letting the partition between the study room and the main room hide me. No one minded. No one cared. No one ever knew I was there.

But now, the bookshelf is gone, and the seat removed. My area is invaded by a double-seated sofa backed up against the wall. As soon as I entered, I stopped and stared at the loss of my hidey hole. Steeling myself not to walk out, I perched on the far end of the sofa and prayed that no one would sit with me. I'm no longer hidden. If anyone looks over, they can see me trying not to be seen. My safe haven is gone.

To make up for that fact, every now and then, I allowed myself to look over at Lorcan. His voice gave me tingles just to hear it. I know it's stupid for me to have a crush on the most popular guy in school after everything that's happened. Even if I'm a Marques, I'm what you call a bad egg. What happened to B is my fault. You make one little mistake and that's it, you're no longer part of the in crowd. And now Jude is having some sort of mental breakdown, I really don't know what will become of our family.

Jude.

I still don't know what's going on with him. What could he have done that was worse than what I did to make his parents keep him away from school?

I asked him what happened last night during dinner. Not out loud. I was careful to send him the message discreetly. I heard the ping from his phone and saw him looking down at the screen, so I know he received it. He didn't reply until the next day.

Just stay away from the Dukes.

That's all it says. Six words without any explanation at all.

In the common room though, I couldn't help it, my eyes were drawn to them. For Saskia Duke, Lorcan's sister, is a dark beauty with piercing shards of emeralds for eyes. I found myself staring into even greener ones—the color of freshly-cut-grass on a summer's day—as Lorcan Duke sought me out from across the room.

Carly Earlshore decided at that moment to stand between us, cutting us off. She was laughing, pointing to Lorcan's tie which was crooked again. He scowled and shooed her away, but she proceeded to sit on his lap to redo the knot, much to the delight of the rugby team.

Was he watching me? Or was it a coincidence?

His occasional sidelong glances made me bolder today. There's a reason I went to the common room rather than hide out in a cold classroom throughout lunch. I needed to see if there was something still there, still lingering on between us—a connection. But like any artistic vision I have in my mind's eye, that slips through my fingers whenever I try to recreate it on the blank pages of my notebook, Lorcan is *sometimes* forever beyond my reach.

I ignored the twist at the bottom of my stomach but seeing him fawn all over her made me want to leave.

It's sickening.

Even Saskia was deigning to give her own brother a feral look. She didn't look happy with Carly. Not that her supposed best friend cares, Carly's insides are probably molten with happiness right now at all the attention he's been giving her lately.

Seeing it all up close, I'd had enough. I closed the book I was reading and got to my feet. I was almost at the door when I heard someone say my name.

Hope soared. *Did Lorcan notice me leaving?*

I looked back to see Finn, not Lorcan, peering straight in my direction. He was holding something aloft. For a split second, I thought I was mistaken, and that Finlay was calling someone else. Until I saw what he was holding.

My journal. You, dear dairy. He was holding you.

Dread pooled in the bottom of my already knotted stomach.

"Aurora, you left this behind."

My face flushed. I stammered a reply, although I knew I needed to go over there to get you.

Bright red from top to toe, heart hammering in my chest, I walked back into the room. Everyone's eyes were trained on me.

They were probably wondering what the pretty pink bound journal with a picture of B on the front contained. *Everything. It contains everything.*

Finlay's gaze was almost level with mine given the heels I was wearing. I chose to wear higher ones today after Lorcan's comment about liking them. I was all too aware of the sound they made as I walked across the wooden floor to take back my property.

"What is it anyway?" The room lurched as he peered at the cover and then opened it up. "A diary?"

"No, it's just a notebook." My voice sounded strained, broken. *I am broken.*

"Oh! That's her diary. Read it out, Finn," shouted Carly, the bitch, from across the room. "I'm dying to know what it says."

"Carly." See. Lorcan tried to stop her.

But I was too focused on my book in Finn's hands to appreciate Lorcan coming to my rescue.

"Maybe I will read it. Maybe it'll tell me why you tried to off yourself." Finn sniggered, eyes glazing as he looked me up and down.

"Don't you dare. It's private," I hissed at the little bastard.

The smirk Finn gave me was the only warning I had before he chucked it across the room to Carly. I whirled after it, but Finn grabbed me, fingers digging into my flesh, holding me roughly in place. The book landed at Carly's feet and she snatched it up, moving away from a disapproving Lorcan and into the center of the room.

We'd drawn a crowd by then and the thought of everyone there knowing what was inside my journal had the sick feeling sweeping through every part of my body.

Cece walked in at that moment, gaze flicking back and forth between us. The look she gave me was pure accusatory. "What are you doing, Aurora?"

Lorcan frowned. "She's trying to get her book back. Finn, let her go. Carly, don't be a bitch. Give the girl her diary back."

190

Girl. That's all I am to him.

"Oh, come on, just a peek." Carly's eyes were practically gleaming as she yanked it open. Oh, the pages, she tore a few of your pages.

"Don't." Was all I managed to say.

Cece, my dear sister, finally strode over to Carly, hand out as though asking for the notebook back.

But it was too late.

Carly was already flipping through my artwork. "What the hell. Some of this is fucked up." Eventually, she got to the center pages, making a face "Uh oh. Fucking hell. Lorc, sweetie, I think you've got a stalker."

She held it up so the whole room could see his name and mine inked together across the middle. Finn laughed and Lorcan just stared, stiff as a board.

I even heard Saskia hiss from across the room.

I dragged my eyes away from Lorcan before he could even look at me, and glared at Carly. I didn't try to hide how upset I was.

"Give it back or I'll report you all for bullying," I croaked as tears pricked the back of my eyelids.

Not my best threat but after the suicides, the school has a zero-tolerance bullying policy. I could get Carly and Finn suspended for their little stunt. The whole school would hate me but that wouldn't stop me.

Carly shot a disgusted look my way and dropped the book to the floor. Pages of drawings and writings fluttered out of it like baby birds trying to fly away and failing. "Here you go. Stop crying, you fucking weirdo," is what she said.

Finn let me go and I scrambled over, anxiety crippling my whole body as I tried to breathe and get to my journal before someone else did. The photo of B had fallen out onto the floor along with a few drawings. I quickly scooped them up as the whispers started back up again.

I felt hot. Tears streamed down my face making my vision

blurred. I couldn't even bring myself to look at Lorcan. All I wanted to do was come back to school and be invisible.

If he hates me now….

I know he does. How could he not.

I staggered to my feet, drunk on shame, unable to look anyone in the eye as I dashed out of the common room.

Cece followed me. She grabbed my arm, stopping me from running off. "Aury." Her voice was soft. "Talk to me. Are you alright?"

She used my old nickname. Two years between us and she treated me like a pariah. I guess after what I did to B, I was.

"Oh, now you're concerned. Don't be," I hissed at her. "I won't try to off myself again."

I couldn't even if I wanted to.

I already tried.

TWENTY-TWO

VIOLA

THURSDAY MORNING, I decide I need to take a break from being 'Tory', and drive to my favorite haunt, aka the shooting range, for some highly-focused anger management. It's either that or kick the shit out of the punch bag hanging in my garage.

I need some fresh air, so gunplay it is. As much as I don't like guns, my carbon-fluted Browning hunting rifle is something to be desired. Halfway through a round, I get a message from Jude to meet at a greasy spoon cafe in the village after school.

Fuck School. I'm done with that place.

After a few more rounds of shredding paper targets with hot flying metal, I realize I can't run away from this. That video has solidified it for me. I want to make someone pay for all the fucked-up shit that's happened to these kids.

I head back to Sacred Heart, messaging Jude that I'll meet him at 8 p.m.

It's getting dark when I pull into the church carpark next to the cafe. I'm immediately alert to a scuffle toward the rear. I slow to a crawl a few meters away, lights off but with the engine still running.

From what I can make out, two guys built like steam trains are beating the shit out of someone. One of them has him in a hold while the other slams his fist into his stomach. Their victim is doubled over. I can't see his face...but I recognize the uniform.

And the mop of golden hair.

It's Jude.

One of them reaches into his pocket and pulls out something that glints under the parking lot flood lights.

I don't even bother to park. I'm out of my car before I can even consider what the hell I'm doing. There are some things I hate more than getting caught—and that's missing an opportunity to alleviate some stress.

And I'm fucking stressed right now.

Knifing someone would alleviate that, plus...

Jude may be a dick, but he's one of mine.

There's one camera, but it's pointed at the main parking lot not where the assault is happening. Satisfied that this place is definitely a blind spot, I stalk toward them whilst hitching my skirt up, feeling for the familiar hilt of the dagger strapped to my thigh. The dickheads fucking Jude up aren't even looking at me.

Jude is though. Lip bloodied, eye swollen, he mouths something. He's telling me to run.

I step in real close behind the guy with the switchblade and disarm the fucker, slicing his forearm open. He drops his weapon screaming, the metal pings as it hits the ground just as Jude comes to life and smacks his head back into the nose of the guy holding him.

Jude then reaches into his pocket, pulls out a gleaming hunk of metal with spikes over the top of it, and smashes his fist into the guy's face. Down he goes.

It's like pure poetry.

Some carnal part of me hisses and that fluttery feeling I've always dreamed of having takes hold.

Panting, blood-dripping into his vision, eyes dark and filled with something I recognize in myself, Jude looks at me. "You should go. This is going to get messy."

Of course, it is.

But I adore messy.

I jut my chin at the two jocks moaning, scrabbling to get upright. "I'm staying. Who are these guys anyway?" I ask between breaths.

Jude exhales. "Rival school. They jumped me as I got out of my car—"

He doesn't finish because the guy with the knife is back on his feet.

"You're fucking dead, Marques," he snarls.

Jude doesn't hesitate.

He ducks and rams his duster into the guy's side, but the fucker doesn't go down. He slashes at Jude, making pretty red streaks over my boy's shirt. Clutching the hilt of my knife, I jam my blade into the fucker's leg. The release is immediate as warm blood gushes from the wound. Rage threatens to choke me. It would be so easy to finish him.

But I don't get to…

The world speeds up as Jude hauls me down the side of the church pathway, away from my victim. I look over my shoulder as the guy stumbles after us. He falls at the first step. Blood pooling on the ground as he tumbles forward. He's not dead, but he's fucked.

Completely fucked.

Jude drags me into a boarded-up side building which smells of old books and mold. There's a broken altar in the middle of it, beyond that the empty shell of the church.

"What is this place?" I gasp, looking down. There's blood all over my uniform.

"It's the old bombed out church. Completely derelict," he reassures me. "No one will come in here."

I wet my lips and look at Jude. "You always carry a knuckle duster around with you?"

"You never know when you might need it." The glint in his black eye is fucking sexy as hell.

I snort and wipe my blade on the wool material of my sleeve. My sweater is fucked anyway. I should take it off.

He gives me a strange look as I haul the sweater over my head, slip the five-inch blade back into the leather strap around my thigh, and drop the hem of my skirt so it's hidden from view.

His dark eyes are filled with a newfound respect. "Do you always carry that dagger around with you?"

"You never know when you're going to need to even the score," I say sweetly.

He lunges for me. I'm not expecting the savage kiss, but I don't stop him. After what just happened, after the week I've had, after Lorcan pissed me off.

I'm hungry for it.

We devour each other, his hands all over my body and under my shirt, my hands tangled in his hair. There's blood everywhere. He hisses with pain as I bite his swollen lip. He's different from Lorcan or Dino. He tastes of metal and adrenaline as his tongue sweeps inside my mouth. I moan as he pulls me over to the altar and pins me against the cold surface.

"It's my turn to get a taste of you, Tory," he whispers in my ear, before kissing me into oblivion again.

"Try and I'll gut you," I growl. I draw the line at fucking teenage boys, no matter how mature they appear.

You said that about Lorcan.

This is different.

Is it?

This is Jude. You don't care about him.

My hand flies to my dagger but he's too quick. Under my skirt, he grabs my hand in his, closing his palm around it and the hilt of the knife. Slowly, using my own fist, he eases the blade out of its sheath and draws the blade up my own body.

It feels like my insides are vibrating. Every sense is heightened. Every nerve on edge.

This is what I've been craving.

He kisses my neck down to my collar bone and uses the edge of the blade to slice away the belt of my skirt and to pop off every button of my shirt. My breath hitches, and my heart fucking races like it's going to explode.

As my skirt falls to the floor, he forces my hand still holding the knife down to my lacy pants.

"How wet are you for me? Hmm?" His hand moves mine, so the knife blade glides under the black lace of my thong. "Shall I cut these off?"

I glare at him, breathing hard. I'm dripping wet for him and he knows it. "Don't you dare."

He smirks, eyes full of promise. I don't make a move to stop him. There's a tug and then a waft of cold air.

"We can't stay here," I hiss, unable to stop the need inside from craving this.

"We have a few minutes." He grins in the dark. He lets go of my hand holding the knife and he drops down between my legs, burying his face between my thighs. Warm breath and then a hot tongue licks, teasing me from the inside out. Waves of pleasure pull me under some sort of spell. My eyes flutter closed. I grab his hair with my free hand, holding the blade with the other.

Fuck. Jude Marques is between my legs.

My moans get louder as he brings me to the edge. All reason darts away. My body, a quaking mess, reacts by arching my back. Shivers erupt everywhere against my will.

Finally, I drop the knife.

It clatters to the floor.

And I come over and over as Jude devours me from the inside out.

· · ·

I blink my eyes and glance around, seeing the abandoned church as I come to my senses. I don't have much faith in religion, but I can appreciate a stark set of rules to live your life by. It's how I determine risk, and how I avoid getting caught.

All this risk is going to get me caught. I'm so far down the rabbit hole, I'm starting to see everything upside down.

I need to stop letting these boys distract me. And Jude is just that— a distraction. I'll admit a very pretty one.

"We need to go," I say to Jude as he comes back up to kiss me, his lips fragrant and warm. He leans close, raging hard on between my thighs promising more than a kiss. My body shivers in anticipation, and since I'm wearing hardly anything below the waist.

Jude nods, reluctantly pulling away, shoving his blazer at me. "I'll grab your car."

Minutes later, there's the sound of an engine outside. I gather my fallen clothes and get into the passenger side. I don't really care if I get blood on the leather, this is Dante's car.

"I'll pick mine up in the morning," Jude says as he handles the vehicle around the twisting, country lanes without slowing down. He's the worst driver in the world.

He looks over at me, hair disheveled, blood spray on his collar. "I'm surprised you showed up tonight."

"Why wouldn't I?"

"After I assaulted you in the hallway, I wasn't sure you'd trust being alone with me."

"You're not dangerous, Jude."

"How do you know?"

"I just know."

After a few minutes, I break the sweet silence. "What did you want to talk about?"

He glances over at me. "Cecilia told me everything."

"And?"

"He's not who you think he is. Lorcan's—"

I purse my lips. "I already know who he is," I say.

He glares my way between keeping his eyes on the road and tapping out a message on his phone. "Because you read Aurora's diary?"

"Eyes on the road, lover boy," I chide at him. "No, because he told me."

He snorts. "Lor tells you what you want to hear. That's his gift."

"And what's your gift?"

He wets his lips. The smile on his face is the Devil incarnate. "Fucking."

"Humble, aren't you?" I say, paying attention to the route Jude is taking me. He's taking me to the house I rented in Victoria's name.

After a few miles, I ask him outright. "How do you know where I live?"

He smirks. "I tracked your car, remember. Your other car. Not this one."

He parks outside the house and turns the engine off. His hands run through his hair, eyes seeking me out in the low-lit car. "Lorcan's been my best mate since kindergarten. He's saved my life once or twice. I owe the fucker. So whatever my uncle is paying you, I'll triple it if you kill him instead."

"That's what this is about? You want to hire me to take out Carl Marques?"

"He didn't give a fuck about his daughter, Aurora. He's just using her death as an excuse to get what he wants—his hands on the inheritance."

"And what makes you think I won't just take your money and kill him anyway?"

"Because I see the way you look at him." I must look confused because he chuckles and adds. "You're in love with Lorcan."

One heartbeat. Another heartbeat….

"No, I'm not," I say without a hint of emotion.

"Sure. Anyway, think about it. We'll talk more in the morning when I pick you up."

I'm almost never speechless, but right now I can't think of a single word to say.

After a few seconds, I get out of the car, Jude's oversized blazer covering my modesty. While the cold air plays havoc with my bare ass, I stalk toward my house as Jude speeds off like a maniac on acid.

TWENTY-THREE

JUDE

I'M DEAD. Lorcan's probably going to kill me this time. I knew she was off limits, but I couldn't fucking help myself. I just had to kiss her, taste her, devour her tight, sweet pussy…

Yeah, I'm fucking dead alright.

Totally worth it.

I drive Tory's car back to Cece's house and park up. I don't give a fuck if she's his fucking soulmate or whatever. I've never wanted to bang a girl more. I don't know what his problem is. Since we hit senior year, we share girls all the fucking time. Not once have we fought over any of them, and we're not about to start now.

Maybe she's the one to turn us against each other.

I give a harsh laugh at that thought and open the car door and step out into the driveway.

We're screwed if that's the case.

Fucking screwed.

There's a strange car in the driveway. One I haven't seen before. *Odd.* The lights are off. I check my phone and there's a missed call from Cece. Shit. I usually ring her after school to make sure she's okay. Ever since Aurora died, I've been staying here more often, keeping an eye on her.

Getting my ass handed to me by those Royal Deacon pricks, and then Tory showing up, threw me off fucking course.

Well, no point in ringing her now.

As soon as I walk in the house, I hear voices coming from the study. I pause by the door, but the voices stop. A few seconds later, there's movement and the sound of someone approaching the study door from the other side. Instinctively, I pull back around the far end of the hallway.

My uncle exits the room, followed by a tall, broad, dark-haired man in a suit who looks very familiar. They walk to the front door, talking quietly. After a minute or two, he leaves, my uncle following him out the door.

I push into Cece's room and walk over to the window as the blacked-out SUV drives away.

"What the fuck, Jude?" She glares at me. It took her five minutes to open her door after my incessant knocking. Her eyes are tinged red. She's been crying.

"Are you going to tell me what's going on? Why was the Dukes' head of security here?"

"You know as much as I do." She frowns, closing the door. "You look a right mess. What the hell happened?"

I shrug. "Fucking cunts from Deacon happened."

"Is that mostly your blood or theirs?" She asks as she walks past me and into the ensuite bathroom.

"Mostly theirs," I say, taking out my phone. I've no idea why my uncle was talking to Haynes, but it doesn't fucking bode well.

Cece comes out a few minutes later with a first aid kit as I'm dialing Lor's number. She makes me sit and starts dabbing shit on the cut above my eye.

"Come on, come on. Pick the fuck up." It goes through to the answerphone.

"Fuck, he's not answering," I hiss at her. I search for Dino's number and call him instead.

He answers on the first ring. "Did you get it?" Is the first thing Dino asks me.

I get up off Cece's bed and wander toward the window. "She didn't have it. Car's clean. I practically stripped her butt naked. Did you have better luck at the bitch's house?"

"Fuck all inside. No notebook, nothing." He sighs. "I still can't believe Carl hired her to take Duke out. Lor must be feeling fucking livid right about now." He pauses. "Hold on, did you say you stripped her butt naked?"

"You got a problem with that, Sinner?"

I look out to where the hill curves around the bend, and a strip of houses can be seen in the distance. The end one, the biggest belongs to Duke. When we were kids, we used to send messages to each other by flicking the lights on and off. Right now, the lights are all out—no one's home.

"No, but you've got a death wish."

"If I'm remembering correctly, you've been all over her like white on rice since the fucking start."

"That was before I knew what she was, and before she drugged me."

"You'll forgive her, you're fucking soft like that."

"Did you fuck her?"

I don't say anything.

"Lor's going to fucking slaughter you," he sighs down the line.

Where the fuck is Lorcan?

I snort a laugh. "Not if she kills him first."

TWENTY-FOUR

AURORA

24th September

Dear Diary,

Why is it the teacher always glances down her nose at me? Miss Hever—if I recall rightly from the previous years. Middle aged and brunette with distrusting eyes, she'd be pretty if it wasn't for the sour look on her face.

"Aurora Marques," she said the other day, clicking her tongue as she said my last name. "You were meant to be here before the bell? Why are you seven minutes late?"

No more than two minutes, surely? "According to my watch it is 2.02 p.m.?"

"And you're meant to be here at five minutes to two. Not two on the dot or two minutes past. Five to two."

No one told me. So I told her that.

"You would know had you started at the beginning of term

209

like everyone else. Report to the disciplinary director at 6 p.m. sharp later today for your mistake."

Someone remarked on how fucking dumb I was as well as crazy and the whole class barked with laughter.

"Class, pipe down. Get back to your workbooks," Miss Hever snarled.

I was late because I spent the entire lunch break in an empty classroom hiding from the groups of seniors congregating in the communal areas.

After the drama in the common room the other day, there was no way I was going back there. But since we're not allowed to leave school grounds to go out for lunch, I didn't have much choice of where else to go. Not that I have a car anymore to take advantage of being senior. They took that away. No car for Aury. She might drive into a lake again.

Not that I have anywhere to drive to.

So rather than go back to where I was humiliated and have everyone stare, I found somewhere quiet to sit and eat my lunch and read. It was bliss for about forty-five minutes. The only problem is that I was so engrossed in my book, I didn't hear the lunch bell.

As soon as Miss Hever turned away to write her stupid math equations on the board, I took the first empty seat near the front.

"Aurora," someone whispered.

I ignored it and opened my book to the right page.

"Aurora!" This time louder.

I turned around. A paper ball came flying my way and landed wet on my cheek. I jerked away and brushed it off with a yelp, much to the delight of the class. It landed perfectly in the old inkwell, carved into the wood of the desk.

I looked up and around, eyeing the room, hoping to catch whoever threw it. But everyone had their eyes glued to the workbook in front of them. I waited for the teacher to turn around before fishing it out of the wooden hole in my desk. It was slimy between my fingers, covered in spit.

Ignoring the sniggers around me, I opened up the damp bit of paper with shaking hands. Inside was a message scrawled in messy handwriting.

No one wants you here.
Why don't you top yourself properly this time?

Feeling sick to my stomach, I dropped the disgusting strip of paper back into the inkwell where I didn't have to see it. My gut churned and I had a sudden urge to leave the room and to wash my hands and face. As soon as the teacher turned around, I raised my hand.

"Please may I be excused to go to the bathroom?"

She sighed when she saw it was me. "Miss Marques, already?"

"We're allowed one toilet break," I said, quoting the handbook. If she wasn't going to let me go, I was going to report the bitch. It was her choice.

The look she gave me was priceless. "Fine, you may be excused but don't dawdle."

I extracted myself from the wooden contraption called a desk and walked quickly out of the classroom. As soon as I was outside, I could breathe again.

Being here is going to be harder than it looks. Much harder.

Is Jude even going to come back? Am I going to have to endure this all by myself?

I could try and repair things with Cece, but when your own sister hates you…

Before B died, I never got this type of attention. Even after that, my German art school was gossip free. Mostly because no one knew what was going on outside of their own problems, let alone country. Here, in Whitechapel, it's plastered all over the local newspapers.

I can't escape what I did. *How did I ever think that I could?*

Feeling cold and shivery, I hunched my shoulders and walked through the empty passageway, the sound of my shoes echoing off the paving stones. Occasionally, blinds in windows twitched. I wasn't imagining the eyes. Someone was watching me…many someones.

I *really*, *truly*, despise this school.

The bathroom was empty when I entered. I washed my hands straight away, to get rid of whosever saliva it was coating my fingers, and then splashed some cold water on my face.

I was staring at my complexion in the bathroom mirror, giving myself some sort of pep talk, when I heard two girls walk in. From the way they marched, heels tapping loudly, I knew it was two popular girls. And I knew as soon as I saw their faces they weren't here to freshen up.

My first thought was that they've followed me in here.

Carly scowled, flicking her brunette hair when she saw me. "Fuck. If it isn't Looney Tunes."

"Whatever you're going to do, get it over with," I said, raising my eyes to meet theirs as I turned around.

"We're not here for you. We couldn't give two shits about you," said Carly. She looked back at her friend. "I told you this place wouldn't be empty."

The dark-haired girl was Saskia. She had streaks down her face like she'd been crying.

She blinked at me, not quite comprehending. "Why don't you fuck off."

"Are you okay?" I asked, doing nothing of the sort. Instead, I leaned so my back was against the sinks, holding on to the rims.

"Do I look okay?" Sas snapped out.

"No," I said. "You look like shit."

The corner of her lips curled. "Your bastard cousin's fault. Told him that if he ever shows his face here again, I'll fucking carve it off."

What the hell did Jude do to make Saskia Duke hate him so much?

I raised a brow. "That's a bit extreme, isn't it?"

Saskia merely frowned. "Says you?"

She's got a point.

"What did Jude do?" I asked, bolder then.

"He cheated on me, that's what."

What the hell? My eyes narrowed and I clutched the cool enamel of the sink behind me a little harder. Of all things, I wasn't expecting that. My perfect cousin dating the most evil bitch in school? *So much for his lofty morals.*

"I didn't even know you were a couple," I said, keeping my voice even.

Carly, eviscerating me with her eyes, glanced at her best friend like she couldn't believe Saskia would openly tell me that.

Saskia rolled her eyes. They glistened under the artificial light. "Why the hell would we be a couple?" For all her bravado, there was the unmistakable sound of her voice breaking as the tears started to fall.

This was a side of Saskia no one got to see. I guess I was now in some sort of twisted world where the other Duke, the cruel one, had a heart. It kind of knocked me for six.

Carly glared my way, as though it was all my fault, and drew Saskia into a protective embrace. "Brilliant. Just brilliant. You can fuck off now."

I left the bathroom quickly then, letting the door swing shut behind me. The sound of Saskia sobbing echoed out into the hall. It was enough to make me shudder.

As I reflected on what just happened, rounding the outer walkway, I saw someone in the distance talking on the phone, leaning against the outside of the building. I carried on walking, getting closer, and my breath caught as I recognized who it was. Cocking his head, rubbing the back of his neck and staring off into space, it was the *other* Duke.

Lorcan Duke.

He didn't see me at first. I caught snippets of his conversation as it drifted through the air.

"...don't understand. What are you saying?" He shifted, brow furrowed, looking confused. "Are you breaking up with me?"

I faltered to a stop, mouth hanging open. Did I just witness Lorcan Duke getting ditched?

As though sensing my approach, he stiffened and looked back, frown deepening as soon as he saw me standing there gaping at him. Heat flamed my entire body. Lorcan Duke caught me eavesdropping on his most private conversation.

"Hold on, Kat. There's someone here." Casually, he hung up, pocketed his phone, and peeled himself from the building he'd been leaning against, never taking his eyes off me. I was so fucked. I wanted to run and hide.

"I'm sorry, I was just..." I didn't finish. I started walking again, carrying on down the pathway to where the door was and escape beckoned. Lorcan strolled after me, blocking my exit.

"Aurora?" He angled his head, eyes narrowed. "Were you listening just now?"

He said my name.

"I didn't hear anything."

His eyes burned into me, seeking out the lie. A slight breeze blew against my bangs, ruffling the edges of our clothes, and teasing the ends of my hair. Eventually, he sighed, drawing in a breath and shoved his hands into his pockets so the thumbs poked out the top. He gave me the saddest smile, enough to make my own heart break all over again.

"Breakups. Who the fuck needs them?"

His admission gave me the courage to keep on looking at him, taking in the straight cut of his nose, the sharpness of his cheekbones, and the way his eyes roamed over me.

Lorcan Duke was the epitome of male beauty.

And he was looking right at me.

Like I existed.

"She doesn't know what she's lost." I said it because it was true. Lorcan, for all his virtues, was dating a Russian mafia princess. I wondered why she broke up with him and it must have shown on my face because he indicated with his head.

"Are you going back to class? Do you have time for a walk?'

Take a walk with Prince Charming himself? Why not.

We walked through the outer grounds of the school and no one bothered us. It might have been because Lorcan was a prince at Sacred Heart or it might have been because everyone else was occupied in class. Whatever it was, it was absolute bliss for a moment. To be there with him and not anywhere else.

We ended up stopping where the path disappeared off into the fields that surrounded the lake.

The wind blew again, and I reached up to brush my hair out of my eyes. He leaned toward me. I wasn't expecting him to grab my wrist hard and turn my palm upwards, exposing the scars.

His grip was vice like and there was a look in his eyes that I'd seen before when we used to sneak off to satisfy each other in the middle of the school day. A hungry, feral look that reminded me of a wolf. A dark thrill of fear shot up my spine as he traced my scars with his thumb and looked at me like he wanted to eat me.

"You did this?" he asked, like it was an obvious question to ask someone who tried to kill themselves.

"You know I did," I said, snatching my arm back as soon as he released me.

"Because of Byron or because of me?"

The intensity of his gaze had my heart palpitating.

Byron. Just saying his name in my mind has the hurt resurfacing, bringing with it all the lost little voices that won't shut up. After he died, I lost control, and everything changed. Lorcan had his eyes on his Russian, Cece blamed me for what happened, and I hated myself. I got in my car and drove to the middle of nowhere. *Alone.* I wanted my death to mean something, when in fact it meant nothing at all.

Because I'm nothing at all.

"Because of you," I choked out after a pause.

Lorcan blinked rapidly, regaining composure. "Let's go into the boathouse."

I allowed Lorcan to steer me across the grass to one of the exterior doorways next to the pier. My mind was rapidly going over everything, coming up with all the reasons why this felt off.

"There was a rumor going around…" Lorcan started once we got inside the boathouse. The whole place was dark and cold, making my skin crawl. This was where it sometimes happened.

My eyes glanced around and then finally settled on Lorcan. "What rumor?"

His green eyes were full of arrogance. "That you tried to kill yourself because of me. I didn't want to believe it."

I hate that rumor. I hate it because it's true. I've no idea how it got out. It's like someone peeled away my skin and looked inside my soul. That Lorcan is even saying it out loud withers away all the love I have for him.

"I just didn't want to lose you," I said, wrapping my arms around myself, admitting some of it but not all. "You kicked me out of the inner circle."

"Jude asked us to keep you out of it. After Byron, he said you weren't yourself."

"What else did Jude say?"

"That you were better off if we kept you from the vote."

My eyes blazed. "He doesn't know what he's talking about. Losing you nearly killed me."

He ran his hand through his hair. "No. That's not true. You don't want this."

"I want it. I can't take it anymore if you shut me out."

He didn't say anything for the longest time.

"Lorcan?" I whispered.

"Strip," he said softly, that feral look was coming back into his eyes.

"What? No." I gave him an incredulous, almost embarrassed, look.

"If you think you can handle it. Take your clothes off," he

216

drawled again, advancing over to me. I stepped back and he captured me in his gaze, wolf eyes all hooded and languid. He was close enough that I had to tilt my head up to look at him. I retreated another step until I was pressed against the hulls of the rowing boats stacked up, lining the interior.

There's nowhere to run.

I shook my head. "No."

He gave a shrug, eyes glazing over as he took the length of me in. "Hitch up your skirt then and turn around. That works too. Unless you can't handle it."

I scowl at him. "Of course, I can. I'm not made of glass."

"Do you want to fuck me or not?"

The way he said it had my tongue darting out to wet my lips. I gave into the nod.

His hands came either side, trapping me between him and the boats.

He kissed me. And I let him, allowing his lips and tongue to sear me, taking my breath away, stealing whatever chance I had to say no.

I'm drowning in the memory of his kiss and feel of him pressed against me even now. *Oh, how I've missed Lorcan Duke kissing me.*

Leaving me wanting more, he pulled back. "See, you do still want me."

"Of course I do," I said, though it was only a whisper. "It was you who discarded me."

"Then let me show you how much I need you." He bent down, breath warm on the shell of my ear. "Turn the fuck around."

I was frozen in place, until his hand slid between my legs. As he stroked me, my breathing hitched, and my toes curled. Inside, I was molten fire.

A moan pulled from my throat and he dropped his other hand to undo his fly. "Turn around. Hitch up your skirt."—He licked the side of my neck— "Or do I have to do it for you?"

Blinking, wetting my lips, I turned around and braced against the hull of the nearest boat. There was a cold breeze on my ass cheeks as my skirt was bunched up around my waist, and my panties were pulled aside. The hardness of him pushed between my legs.

"Fuck, Aury, you're dripping wet," he groaned, pushing harder.

"Fuck me the way I like it."

Dirty.

He grabbed my hair and jerked my head back exactly the way I needed it. My eyes fluttered closed, and I shuddered at the sensation of him spearing me from behind, slick and tight. Quivered at the way his hand wrapped around my hair, pulling me back so I could hardly gasp air.

It was like he was owning me, using me, and discarding me all at the same time.

As much as I hated this feeling, I craved it too. I still do.

Only if he'd restrained me to the boats, would I have enjoyed it better.

What has he done to me?

A thousand thoughts scattered from my mind as I clutched onto the side of the boat and Lorcan Duke fucked me savagely over it. His strokes were hard and deliberate, filling me up, taking all the air from my lungs so I could hardly breathe. Taking everything away from me until there was nothing left.

And I could pretend for a few stolen moments that the whole of last year never happened.

This is what I want. This is how much I need him.

I love Lorcan Duke. And hate him.

And I can't tell a single soul.

TWENTY-FIVE

VIOLA

WHAT IS *it with people waking me up in the middle of the night?*

I scan the caller ID. It's only Dante so I make him wait while I answer it.

"What the fuck did you do to Pierre?" he asks in that matter-of-fact way of his.

"He was in my way. Why are you calling me at this hour?" I say as I stare at the wall, blinking and yawning. There are no birds singing outside yet, so it must be super fucking early still.

"Because there's a van with a dead body in it sitting in my driveway and I'm about to go to work."

"You like to clean up," I remind him.

"And what's this about a notebook?" he sighs.

I sent him a message last night before I passed out about the notebook.

"The last dead body you cleaned for me. There was a notebook in her pocket."

"Now why would I keep any evidence?"

"So, you don't have it?"

"No."

"Why not?"

"Because I burned the fucking body and everything on it."

I get dressed into a black hoodie, black leggings, and matching running shoes, and drive over to Dante's cabin. All the lights are off as they should be. Leaving my car parked and tucked out the way, I do a quick search through his things. Dante wouldn't usually keep anything from a mark, but he might have if it looked important, and notebooks usually are.

I search all the places I can think of, and I'm about to give up when I see a familiar manila folder. It is the type Polina uses to send us jobs in. I go over and open it up, mainly because I'm nosy. Inside is an identical file to the one I received at the start of the Duke job, only this time there's information on me too, including my cover story, my cause for being at the school.

There's only one reason Polina would give us an updated file with information about another contract killer inside it. Because they've been added as a fucking target.

I look around and spy the courier envelope the file came in. It's in the trash beside the desk. I pull it out and check the time and date on it.

Dante received the file just before he called me.

And he said he was off to work.

I drop the envelope back into the trash but not before spotting what's under the envelope—it's a little black notebook. I fish it out of the can and pocket it just as my phone rings. It's not someone calling. It's a notification from the tracker app I have installed. Lorcan's car is on the move.

I stare at the flashing dot that represents my boy's Bugatti, registering that it's moving closer to his house. Almost inside it. Like he parked it in the garage.

My chest tightens and my skin tingles all over. It's a feeling I've come to associate with wanting to do extreme violence.

Dante wasn't calling me to complain about Pierre. He was calling me to check I was at fucking home.

I get to Lorcan's house when it's still dark. I park off the main road and use the low light to slip around the back of the house and break into one of the downstairs rooms through a window. It's pitch black inside too, but once my eyes have adjusted, I find my way around by remembering the layout. And it doesn't take me long to locate the inner garage door.

Fumes ravage my throat as I yank open the door. Lorcan's car is sitting idle with the engine on, filling the entire room with exhaust smoke. Through the hazy smoke, I see someone inside.

Covering my mouth and nose with my hoodie, I dash into the garage, pull open the door and switch off the engine. I drag Saskia out of the car and into the main house. She's barely conscious but she's breathing.

"Lorcan," she wails, hacking up her lungs vehemently, eyes fluttering between open and closed.

"Where is he?" I demand.

She shakes her head, tears staining her cheeks, coughing hoarsely as she curls up on her side. "I don't… know. He…took him."

He. Dante.

I run back to my car, open the trunk and take out my crossbow. Adrenaline peaking all over the place. I drive quickly to my apartment. If I know Dante, he doesn't like to waste time. He's the type to kill two birds with one stone—me and Lorcan being the fucking birds in this case.

The sight that greets me in my own bedroom is interesting, to say the least. Lorcan is alive—tied up and gagged, but alive. All of my killing tools are laid out next to the bed. There's even a load of plastic sheeting on the floor. The centerpiece being Lorcan as the main sacrifice.

Dante has recreated my fucking kill room.

Lorcan sees me and his eyes flash with something, they dart behind the door where I know Dante is most likely hiding.

I pull in a deep breath.

I tread carefully into the room, my crossbow pointed at the door. "Come out, Dante," I snap. "Don't make me ruin the door so I can't get the deposit back."

My mentor gives me a dangerous smile as he steps out into view with his trademark weapon of choice—a gun with a silencer pointed right at me.

"V—" is all he gets to say before I shoot him in the stomach. *Don't bother with chit-chat. Get in and out. Ironic, Dante was the one who taught me that.*

The fucker goes down, stumbling, but not before he pulls his trigger. I duck to the floor, and he misses by fucking millimeter. Soft gunshots zip past my ear, thudding into the wall behind me.

So much for that fucking deposit.

I crawl behind the bed and reset my bow, wiping my clammy palms on my leggings so I can get a better grip.

Purposely, I aimed for his center of gravity and it paid off. I don't like to think what would have happened had he shot first or aimed a little more to the left.

"I'm just… doing my job, V," Dante hisses between breaths.

"You have fifteen, maybe twenty minutes tops before you bleed out," I say. "Put down the gun and I'll call Quinn to send a medic." I'm lying but it can't hurt to see if he'll fall for it.

"Or I could shoot Duke and we both lose?"

A churning sensation mauls at my insides, matching my rapidly beating heart for attention.

"Shoot him. I don't care," I say, gripping the edge of the bed.

Silence.

"What are you waiting for?" I say louder, adjusting my bow. "Fucking shoot him already."

More silence.

Coldness settles in the base of my stomach.

Why do I feel like this? What is it about this fucking boy that makes me so fucking weak?

I stick my head out around the edge of the bed. Apart from the vibrant bloodstain on the carpet, there's nothing to say Dante was even here. *Should I go after him?*

No.

He saved my life once.

And now we're even.

But I do have to fucking uproot my life all over again. If I keep adding to the people who aren't supposed to find me, changing countries as often as underwear, I'm going to end up in Australia at this rate.

Lorcan's usually impassive gaze is wary, like I might just shoot him with my bow. *Not a bad idea.* I give him a dispassionate look, sizing him up, and then drop the bow. I wrestle my dagger from my wrist sheath and start slicing through the knots that are holding him down. Then I toss him his clothes and the notebook.

His beautiful green eyes catch mine. "You found it?"

"Just get dressed. We're leaving," I say, walking out of the room.

I take Lorcan to my *real* apartment. It's risky bringing him here, but I'm leaving this place after tomorrow. It will do for one night. Dante doesn't know where I live, just as I don't know where he retreats to late at night. He only knew the address of my cover story house because I let him deliver the loaner car there.

This is what happens when you allow people to see where you sleep. They turn up and try to fucking kill you.

"So, this is where you actually live?" Lorcan asks, ending his brief phone call to Saskia as we pull up.

"Is your sister okay?" I counter as we exit the car.

"She's fine. She's going to spend the rest of the week at a friend's house," he says as he follows me inside.

I nod, switching off the code for the alarm. I don't actually care about his sister. Old habits are hard to break. Years of pretending to be the same as everyone else, of blending in and not standing out, makes me say and do things I don't mean to avoid being alienated. It's what I've had to do for survival. Right now, though, I'm tired and I'm on fucking autopilot. I'll probably start asking if he wants a cup of tea next.

"You can have the couch. I'm showering and then I'm going to bed. It's late," I say without flourish.

Lorcan looks around and then nods. I grab him a blanket and then leave him to it.

I'm finally drifting off to sleep but a *hush-hush* noise, like someone treading on the thick carpet, wakes me up. In the low light, Lorcan is leaning against the door, watching me with dark, penetrating eyes. He's bare-chested, barefoot, wearing only a pair of jeans. His inky black tattoos camouflage him against the night, making him more beautiful and more predatory than he already is. Only the lone, white square of gauze stuck over his collarbone reminds me how vulnerable he is.

He strolls inside like he owns the place.

"Your sofa is uncomfortable. I'm sharing the bed."

"I should just kill you already, save myself all this trouble," I say, blinking my eyes half-open.

"If you were going to kill me, you would have done it already," he says, his tone is intense and teasing as he comes up beside me.

And then he does what I really want him to do deep down— he climbs into the bed and straddles me, running his hands through my hair. My gut reaction is to head-butt him and smack his nose into his fucking skull, breaking it. But it's been a long day. I don't have the energy to fight him.

He's also turning me the fuck on.

"Don't get cocky, Duke," I say.

"Much prefer the blonde," he drawls, ignoring my comment,

continuing to wrap my hair around his fists. "Glad you got rid of that hideous wig."

I slap his hand away. "Don't fucking touch me."

His eyes flash with anger. He grabs my wrists and hauls them above my head.

"I said don't touch me," I hiss as he restrains me easily with one hand. He's not gentle as he does it, and he grunts in pain when he moves his damaged shoulder higher than he should. His eyes drink the sight of me wearing nothing but a pair of cotton panties.

"And I told you, you owe me. I don't care if you stab me, I'm going to fuck you right here, right now," he says, stoically. The sight of him towering over me, scars and angry red lines marring his perfect form, I feel breathless. Heat pulses between my legs.

Fuck. *I want him.*

Holding me down with one hand, he opens his belt buckle and unhooks it from his jeans. Then he loops the ends around my wrists and attaches it to the bed, fully restraining me.

"You're going to regret this," I promise him.

He smirks. "I'm going to fuck you hard and cum inside you, and there's nothing you can do about it. Nothing to regret about that."

He stands up to shrug off his jeans and boxers and then lowers himself down. His body is warm, hot almost. The cedar scent of him invades my senses as he tears into me with a kiss, hands and lips teasing.

Then he moves down, yanking my knickers off, positioning himself so he can bite and suck on my inner thighs. He finds my clit, and laps at it. His teeth are dangerously close to where I need him to be as his tongue plunges into my core, tasting. His hand brushes and probes against my rear entrance, making me squirm. Finally, he eases his fingers and his thumb inside both holes, using my own wetness as lubricant.

"What the hell...are you doing?" I ask.

He ignores my question and squeezes around my G-spot,

sending pulses of pure pleasure rippling through my entire body. Until I'm desperately clawing at the bed I'm tied to. Until my body shakes, and I'm moaning louder.

I can't help it.

"Music to my fucking ears," he drawls before consuming me with his mouth again, bringing me to the edge, taking me to that place between heaven and hell.

I orgasm hard. Too hard.

I very nearly knee him in the face, but he grips my thighs and holds them wide open.

"Oh no you don't. I'm not finished with you yet."

Still holding me down, he comes up to where I'm seething. I struggle against his leather belt, chafing my skin. I want to smack the smirk on his lips away.

I also want him to fuck me raw, but I'll never confess that in my lifetime.

"Stop frothing at the mouth and admit you're enjoying it, sweetheart."

"Once I get out of this, I'm going to kill you," I snarl.

"You're a shit liar. You're soaking wet." He slips a finger inside and strokes my aching clit to prove a point. "You want me to take you like this. Your eyes are practically begging me to."

"Go to hell—"

He shuts me up with a harsh kiss. I taste myself on his lips as he fucks me with three fingers inside, stretching me until I'm gasping. Then he pulls away and nuzzles my neck. "You're loving this, aren't you?"

"No," I rasp the lie.

His thick, hard cock throbs as it lies against my thigh. He pushes at my entrance. "I'm going to stick my dick in you now, sweetheart. Be a good girl and take it."

"I probably won't even feel it," I say acidly.

The smile he gives me is one of the Devil.

Eyes darkening, keeping my legs apart, he thrusts into me with one deep stroke making me shudder. I arch my back. His mouth teases my breasts, biting my nipples, as he fucks me. My own hips find a rhythm with his as I let him abuse my body. Let him own me. Let him consume me. He fucks me until I'm gasping and panting.

As soon as I'm close, with hunger glinting in his deep, green orbs, Lorcan wraps a hand around my throat and presses it closed.

Lack of air burns my lungs and spins me light-headed. Bound and helpless, complete and utter powerlessness overwhelms me. I lose myself in waves of pleasure as they shiver up my spine. As Lorcan seals my mouth in a kiss, he releases his hot load inside me with a wicked smile and teasing groan.

Later, lying in a mess of tangled sheets and limbs, Lorcan strokes my hair while I flip through the notebook. I slept for three hours before the sun got to me and stirred me awake. School started two hours ago but neither of us makes any move to get up.

I'm so done with fucking school.

"There are over two hundred names in this damn book," I say. It's also more of an appointment book with names and dates.

"Joseph wanted Blair to keep track of every client."

"Do you always call your father by his first name?" I ask him.

He sighs behind me. "He's not my actual father."

"Fair enough," I say, flicking through the pages until I get to the date labeled in Aurora's own diary as 'dirty'.

Three names are entered. One name is Aurora's, the second is the teacher from the common room, and the third is Sacred Heart's very own slimy headmaster.

On the opposite page is the same kind of entry but this time Lorcan's name is substituted for Aurora's.

I stare at the names. Lorcan has stopped stroking my hair.

"Come on," I say, placing the book on the bedside table, getting out of bed. "We're late for your diabolical excuse of a school."

TWENTY-SIX

LORCAN

THE ANGEL IS SPRAWLED out like a feast before me, flicking through the notebook like it holds all of God's secrets.

It may as well do. *It holds my father's.*

"There are over two hundred names in this damn book," Viola says.

Viola. I can't get used to calling her that.

"Joseph wanted Blair to keep track of every client," I say, tracing her divine body with my fingertips, making her shiver a little. She's like a wild thing that needed to be tamed. I keep waiting for her to snap, or bite me, or do something savage. But she hasn't yet. It's a miracle she's letting me touch her right now. I'm so used to her threatening me that I can't quite fucking believe it.

She glances at me, exotic almond-shaped eyes peering back into mine. "Do you always call your father by his first name?" she asks.

I let out a deep breath, running my hands through her silky, soft hair. "He's not my actual fucking father." The urge to wrap its length around my fist and yank her head back is fucking over-whelming. She hasn't wrapped those pretty lips around my cock yet. The thought of it has my dick pulsing. Fuck, it doesn't take much with her.

Just one stray sinful thought.

"Fair enough." Her brow furrows when she gets to the last few pages. She stares at one of them for the longest time. I stop stroking her hair.

What the fuck is she looking at?

I glance down.

Ah.

It's my name on the page.

For a brief second, my vision darkens, my throat closes up, and the nightmare of my fucking life comes back to haunt me. It's easy to forget for a moment, but then something fucking mundane happens, like your name in a goddamn notebook, and every piece of messed up shit that's ever happened to you comes flooding back.

I should destroy that damn thing.

Next to me, Viola tenses and then sits up. I muse over hauling her back into bed with me, and fucking her all over again. This time slowly, teasing every moan and every pleasure from that tight, toned little body of hers.

But I'm too late.

"Come on." She places the book on the bedside table and gets out of bed. "We're late for your fucking diabolical excuse of a school."

Later then, wild thing. I've caught you now.

I drop Viola off at the front of the school and pull over, leaving the engine running. The plan I've wanted to pull off my entire fucking life all comes down to this point. Would I have done it if I hadn't met her? Probably. Would I have failed? Most fucking likely. Joseph is not to be underestimated.

I should know.

He fucking raised me to be exactly like him.

My phone rings. It's Saint. I pick it up.

"So, she didn't kill you?" Jude asks.

"Does it sound like I'm dead?"

"Ah fuck, I owe Sin a grand. I thought she'd have put a bullet in your head by now just for trying to blackmail her."

"You still don't trust her do you."

"Nope. And I think it's a bad idea bringing her in."

I don't mention that she saved my life last night. Maybe I want to keep that to myself.

"It was bring her in, or get rid of her and I don't know about you but I'm sick and tired of killing innocent girls."

He snorts. "She's hardly fucking innocent."

"Even better," I snap. "Now put Dino on. He's there, right?"

"Lor, what's up?"

"Did you move it? Was it in the safe like I said?"

"All done and dusted."

"And the house?"

"One frat house in your offshore company name coming up."

"Just make sure the security system is top of the range," I say, and then hang up.

I'm not having that psycho break in again. Sas nearly fucking died last night. A coldness runs through me at that thought. It brings me back to what I'm doing here…bringing my own angel of death right to the *heart* of the fucking problem.

My angel of death.

How apt. Just how long I can keep her on a leash for is another *fucking* problem for another *fucking* time.

I ignore the twist in my gut and adjust my mirror so I can see her as soon as she exits the building. I believe her when she says her tech girl disabled all the cameras. I believe her when she tells me she won't double-cross me.

Why?

Because in Blair's apartment, I found an older, identical-looking notebook with the same codings that the network my father runs uses. And it had Viola's name in it, scrawled across more pages than I could fucking count.

TWENTY-SEVEN

AURORA

30th September

Dear Diary,

It's just a school. *A school full of sharks looking for their next meal.*

That may be true, but what's the worst that can happen? I've been bullied by my own family my entire life. What could the students at this school possibly do to me that's any worse than what I've already had to endure.

Nothing. Except maybe death.

I'm not scared of dying. It'll be a release from this non-existent life that's for sure. After B died—dying hasn't seemed like such a leap.

The words swim off the page until I wrangle them back. I try to refocus on what I'm supposed to be doing, reading instead of thinking of my dead brother.

Breathe, Aurora.

To avoid ever setting foot in the common room again, I've

been setting up camp in the basement during lunch. I liked the classrooms but occasionally a teacher would find me and ask me to leave. It's against the rules to be in some parts of the school alone but there's no way in hell I'm ever going back to the common room.

At least the music rooms in the basement are used by no one. They're blessedly empty now that everyone prefers to use the music rooms in the new building since it was built. No one comes down here. *Ever.*

Not even Lorcan.

Word has gotten out. Lorcan Duke, the most eligible bachelor in the whole school, is no longer taken. He's fair game and from the way most of the girls in the school are drooling over him, he won't be single for long.

The memory of yesterday surfaces. After he fucked me in the boathouse, he told me to be at his party on Saturday, and then turned and walked away leaving me wondering if we were back to being together in secret or if he was just using me.

It's that thought that fluttered through my mind as I settled down to read my book.

"Are you sure there's no one down here?"

I stopped reading. My shoulders tensed as I tried to work out who it was.

"I'm sure. No one comes down here."

There was a set of footsteps on the stairwell and the sound of the door to the larger music room at the end of the corridor opening. As I came out of the smaller room, I should have taken that as my chance to slip by whoever it was and take to the stairs; however, the murmur behind the large music room door had me walking up to it. I placed my ear against the polished wood and listened. These rooms were meant to be soundproofed. If I could hear them, they must have been shouting.

"...he's out of control. You said you'd talk to him," said one.

Another voice next, deeper. "How was I to know Jude would be there?"

"Because I told you they were screwing. Of course, he was going to be there," the female voice hissed.

"I'm not here to do your dirty work, Saskia. You said you needed someone to take you to the clinic. I can do that. But are you sure that's what you want?"

"Of course that's what I want. It's an abomination. I need to get rid of it," the female voice screeched.

I stepped back. It was Saskia. I shouldn't have been there, listening in.

Before I could stop it, the book I was holding slipped from my grasp and clattered to the floor. Instantly, I froze. There was nothing but silence on the other side of the door.

Knowing I wouldn't make it to the top of the stairs in time, I hurried back to the room I was hiding in. I closed the door trying not to make any noise. Every cell in my body was awake, every nerve riding the edge of sanity.

There was the sound of someone walking into the hall. "Dino, It's Marques. She's down here. Look, this is her book."

I left the fucking book I was reading.

The door to the music room I was in swung open. I stumbled back from it. Saskia scowled as soon as she saw me.

"There you are."

I pushed past her racing for the stairs, but someone was already there. A squeal escaped my lips as I hit a solid chest and a set of broad arms closed around me.

"Hey, hey. Where are you going?" My assailant's voice, low and baritone, tickled as he breathed close to my ear. My body tensed even more when I recognized the voice. Breathing in short gasps, I angled my head to see the boy holding me. And just as my body knew already, my eyes took in Dino Vice holding me prisoner.

"Why are you down here?" He frowned.

I struggled in his steel grasp as his arms crushed me closer to his hard body. "No, no let me go. I'll scream if you don't."

Don't let them smell fresh blood?

239

What a crock of shit.

"Go ahead and scream, darling. This whole place is sound-proofed," Saskia said to me, as she approached.

"Don't do this. Let me go."

She tilted her head. "Do what? What do you think we're going to do?" She looked at Dino. "See, she's fucking bonkers. Bring her in here."

I opened my mouth and screamed as Dino dragged me toward the empty music room at the end of the hall, the large one with desks stacked up on one side. The door closed and I could hear the click of the lock.

Where were the teachers? Where was everyone else? This place couldn't have been that sound-proofed? I screamed like a banshee.

Deep down, I knew the truth.

No one was coming.

"Now will you stop struggling, if I let you go?" Dino asked me, sounding sincere.

"Get the fuck off me, you pervert," I screamed at him, and managed to bite the bare arm he was holding me with.

He released me pretty quick. "Jesus, Aury. What the fuck is wrong with you? Why is Lorcan even entertaining bringing her on Saturday? She's not well."

Why does everyone keep saying that?

I was too busy worrying about Dino to pay attention to Saskia. I only knew she was there because I suddenly heard her talking. "I don't fucking know. I've got enough to worry about. Like Jude cheating on me."

"Sas, this is serious."

"Urgh fine. I'll speak to Cece. Maybe she can keep her sister under control. Stop screaming, no one can hear you down here."

I clamped my mouth shut and shot her a dark, angry look. She was right. No point in wasting my energy screaming again.

"What do you want to do with her?" Dino asked.

Saskia's eyes were dancing like she was on something. "Jude

cares about her, right? Maybe he'll come on Saturday if she's there."

Dino behind me, gave a harsh laugh. "You expect he'll come running after he sees what we've done to his precious little cousin?"

Saskia glared at him. "Oh, he had better. I'm growing tired of waiting for him to show his cowardly fucking face. And this one thinks she can whore herself out to my little brother? She needs to know her place."

They were talking about Jude, and talking like I was just a pawn in the middle of some fucking game that the Dukes were playing with my family.

I drew in a breath and focused on Saskia because she was in front of me and because she seemed to be the leader in this strange pairing. My mouth was dry, and my heart was trying to beat its way out of my chest. Still, I managed to stare her down the entire time.

"What are you going to do to me?" *Don't you know already? They're going to kill you.*

Saskia smirked. "Oh, I'm not going to do anything to you, lovely. You're going to do it to yourself. I mean, look at you, you're a wreck. I bet you kill yourself by the end of the week."

"No, I won't," I snap.

"Yes, you will." She leaned in close, grabbing me roughly by the neck so she could whisper into my ear. "You killed your own brother, no wonder you want to slit your own pretty little throat."

It was a car accident. I hadn't meant to drive into the lake.

"Sas, too harsh," Dino chided from behind.

Somewhere in the distance, a bell tolled.

Lunchbreak was over.

Saskia sighed and dropped her hand away. Her eyes softened, losing the otherwise manic look, and she glanced at the delicate watch on her wrist. "Fuck. I have a class to be at."

"Wait, so that's it?" I heard Dino ask.

Saskia looked over my head at him. "What did you expect?"

Dino's body tensed. "You're a right bitch sometimes, Sas. You know that."

And then he stormed out, leaving me alone with her.

Saskia sighed and looked at me coldly. "Dino's right. Don't come on Saturday. Stay away from my brother." And then, without looking back, she left the room letting the door fall shut behind her.

After I got home, I told Jude about what happened. Cece was in her room crying again. Jude shouted at me for disobeying him and banned me from going to Lorcan's party. I honestly don't know who he thinks he is. I'm going. And I'm going to wear something nice.

Fuck Saskia and to hell with Jude. They think I can't handle it anymore after what happened. I'm not broken.

I just want it to be like it was.

I want all things back the way they were.

Lorcan and I together, and everyone not treating me like I'm made of fucking glass!

TWENTY-EIGHT

VIOLA

I'M SITTING OUTSIDE in the corridor wearing my super short school uniform as the receptionist looks up.

She smiles. "You can go inside now, he'll see you."

I smile coyly and enter, making sure to look a little uncertain. The heavy door closes behind me, shutting me inside the headmaster's office. A middle-aged, overweight, balding man looks up from his desk.

"Ah, Victoria, how lovely to finally meet you."

"Headmaster Thompson. The pleasure is all mine," I say, showing my teeth, as I walk over to shake his hand.

I waste no time.

Pulling the needle full of Vicodin out from my blazer pocket, I jam it in his throat before he can scream. And as he slips into a dreamless sleep, I take my time restraining him to his chair, naked from the waist down.

The Naloxone brings him round with a start. His unfocused eyes settle on me, taking in my nubile body almost bursting out of my tight uniform, and my youthful fresh, and innocent looks. I look like the wettest dream and the hottest fantasy. He has no idea the kind of nightmare I can be.

I'm straddling him, playing with his pathetic excuse of a micropenis. It's starting to get hard. I push down the revulsion as he drinks me in with desperate, perverted eyes.

I don't want to wait for foreplay.

I lean in to whisper in his ear. He mumbles around the gag in his mouth. Fear mounts in his eyes as he sees the predator rise within me. The blackness that's waited so long for release rises up and the mask falls away.

"Aurora sends her regards," I say sweetly.

I take his silver letter opener from the desk and slash the shaft of his softening dick open from tip to groin. Blood sprays in a hot arc coating us, the chair, and the walls around us, as I continue my work.

He gives a muffled scream.

The light in his eyes fades quickly.

He couldn't even get hard for me.

I exit the office. The receptionist is nowhere to be seen; sent away on an errand. Down the hallway, Saskia is waiting with a spare set of clothes. She hands them to me, and we exchange nods. If the blood bothers her, splattered all over the spare uniform she lent me, she doesn't show it.

I head to the nearest girls' bathroom to change into a pair of ripped jeans, my boots, a strapless top, and my leather jacket. I ditch the wig and the lenses, taking care to wash the visible blood from my face and my hands.

Outside, a Bugatti is waiting, purring like a kitten in the sunlit courtyard. I trot down the steps as the door opens. I slide inside.

"It's done," I say.

Lorcan gives me a sexy, appreciative look and drives like a maniac through the school grounds and up the long winding driveway, away from Sacré-Cœur Preparatory School towards

London. In my back pocket is the notebook full of names. I pull it out and open it up to the page with the corner bent. I cross off one name, and then I turn the page to circle the next one.

Eventually, we drive past the area where Dante's cabin was. Smoke fills the air. Someone lit a fire recently and it wasn't me.

"Turn in here and pull over," I say to Lorcan. If he remembers this place it doesn't show on his face. He just drives me to where I want to go. At the end of the drive in the clearing where the farmhouse once stood, is a pile of hulking ash and smoke. The entire place was scorched from this earth last night after I failed to kill him. I can't see him coming back and setting the place alight. He must have had a failsafe somewhere. A remote accelerant he could trigger that he's always had in play.

Or.

Dante fucking knew.

Lorcan stops the car a good few meters away. In the footwell is my crossbow. I take it with me as I slip out of the Bugatti while my boy turns the car around.

Walking around the edge, I see nothing to indicate Dante is still lurking. He's gone. Vanished.

I reach inside but I come up empty. I don't know what I was expecting. Sadness. Anger. Regret. But there's nothing. It's like I'm not even human. Dante was the one person I trusted. The one person who had my back. And look what he fucking did. And yet, I feel only an itch under my skin that we need to keep moving and a slight irritation that my killing place is no more.

What does that make me? Dead inside? *A monster like my father said I was?*

A monster like him?

Fuck that. I close all the unreasonable, unhelpful thoughts down. And with a sigh, I walk back to the car.

Dante, you sly bastard.

Of course, he'd disappear too. The only thing that niggles me about that is from now on I'll have to clean my own kills. You know how much I fucking hate cleaning.

We carry on driving, occasionally Lorcan glances my way. I return the gaze, trying again to feel *something*. Jude said that he can tell by the way I look at Lorcan, that I have feelings for him. There's a slight edge that teases through my soul whenever I see him. It's like the beating wings of a bird, soft and fluttery, but also unobtainable. Whenever I try to grab hold of it to study, it flies away like it was never there.

Is that love?

I have no idea.

All I know is, behind his dark glasses are the sorrowful eyes of a killer who has a need to satisfy his darkness. *Just like I do.* He gets me. He understands me. Because he has it too. And that's more than I've ever dreamed of finding in this cold, empty world.

I used to not want to get caught. I used to be careful. I trusted no one.

But now, it's like a fire has been lit within me and it's chasing us into the dark, into the middle of nowhere.

We just need to go fast enough.

And just maybe…

The flames won't catch up.

TWENTY-NINE

DANTE

THE WHITE BLONDE-HAIRED girl on the screen of my phone, crossbow tucked under her arm, climbs into the sports car. A few minutes later, it races out of the clearing. It's an old recording from one of the many nature cams still working in the area. I've watched it a thousand times.

V was visiting the remains of my cabin. *What was she hoping to find?*

I turn off the video by sliding my phone closed and go back to the computer in front of me. A sob to my left makes me look over at the girl trussed up and tied to the chair. Her tear-stained face, hidden by her dark hair, pleads at me.

Quinn. She wasn't expecting me. I didn't hurt her...much. And I did have to gag her to stop her screams. Fortunately for me, she lives alone, there's no one around for miles.

I may not kill her. *I'm only here to borrow her toys while I search for our mutual friend.*

After a few minutes, the screen starts flashing and a count-down timer starts up.

She rigged a failsafe into the system.

I get out of my chair and slowly walk over to where Quinn is tied up. She whimpers as I drag her chair closer to the terminal.

I crouch down in front of her. "Unlock it," I say softly. "If you refuse or try to escape, you won't survive."

It's not a threat. Just the truth.

Unlike V, I don't crave violence, but it doesn't bother me to maim or kill. If I have to end Quinn—despite liking her—for the job, I will.

I let her see that in my eyes, and she nods, sniffing quietly. Quinn knows enough of our world to know I'm not bluffing. Harper Black owns her, and therefore so do I.

I pick up the blade I left on the desk, slice through her bonds, and step back. I don't bother to remove the gag. Quinn works quickly, efficiently, every so often glancing back at me with fear dancing in her eyes.

My phone vibrates to let me know there's a message. I slip it open and read it. It's from Harper Black himself.

> *"No more games. When you find her, bring her home."*

That's it. Nothing else.

Home. To the house where she grew up.

"I'm...It's done," Quinn says, the whites of her eyes paler than usual. She shakes her head, silent tears falling as I approach. "You monsters should leave her alone." Her whisper is barely audible.

She has it wrong. I'm merely the messenger. Harper Black, V's father, is the monster. And he doesn't like not knowing where his family is, because family is the most important thing in this pathetic world.

Viola's just forgotten that.

On the screen is an empty vault showing only the latest message from my ex protégé to her beloved Quinn. She wiped it clean before I got here. Clever girl. But not clever enough. A message can be traced.

Soon.

V, I'm coming for you.

THIRTY

AURORA

1st October

Diary,

I did it. I went to the party. Everyone was looking at me. Lorcan was there and he kissed me in front of everyone. It should have been the happiest day. And it was until those older men showed up. And I knew, I just knew…

Lorcan introduced the old man to me and then left me with him.

Once, he asked me if I was okay to do this, and I lied. I fucking lied because I didn't want to disappoint him.

"Can you do this, Aurora?" Lorcan's clear green eyes begged me to say yes. He needed me to do this. It's not the first time, but after the last time, I thought I would die.

And now…

I told him. "Yes, I can do this."

Not even his sister can do this for him.

Then he left me in the room with the old man. Some head-master at one of the schools. I can't remember which one. Not when he purrs in my ear. "It's just you and me now, beautiful."

"Wait—"

I didn't get to say anything more. Air slammed out of my lungs as he shoved me onto the bed and trapped me with his heavy body. I tried to push him off, but the old man is built like he's made of stone. I'm not going anywhere. *This is really going to happen.*

Could I appeal to his better nature? Could I convince him to let me go?

No.

"You're prettier than your picture, Aurora," he said as he took my wrists and easily pinned me to the mattress. Struggling was useless. I wasn't even moving an inch.

"Please stop," I whined at him. "Don't do this."

"You know I've wanted to do this for a long time." His pale eyes were filled with lust and something darker as he looked me up and down. "I'm going to fucking enjoy this."

I averted my head, but his mouth still managed to lock onto mine. He tasted of mint. It made me gag. His hands, steel bands around my wrists, clamped harder, keeping me immobile. His body still lying on top, crushed me beneath him so I couldn't breathe as he ground me into the bed. His dick, hard, jabbing me in the hip, was the last thing I wanted to feel.

Wetness stings my eyes as I write this. My throat lets out a rasp as I remember.

I'm not strong. I said that to keep Lorcan happy. I wanted to change my mind, but it was too late.

It's much too late now.

It's done.

I closed my eyes and mind during it, letting my thoughts flutter away with the bells chiming as a man, old enough to be my father, ripped off my skirt and pulled down my panties with rough fingers.

The last and only coherent thought to flit through my mind was…

At least I'm not dead.

I made a mistake. There's only one person in this whole world who can make it better. Who can make the pain go away.

Lorcan.

I can't do it. I tried. I'm not strong enough. Not harsh enough. Not enough, full stop.

He'll do it.

For me, he'll make the pain go away.

If he doesn't, then there's only one thing left to do.

I'll tell the whole world that his sister is carrying Joseph Duke's baby, and let's see who breaks apart then.

Because it won't be me.

I'm already broken.

EPILOGUE

VIOLA

I OPEN my eyes to the smell of bacon and the sounds of coffee grinding. The bed is empty but not cold. The scent of him is all around me. He was just here.

I get up and throw on a thin sweater. It's enough to combat the crazy amounts of heating blasting through the house. The boys like it warm.

Blood too rich. They can't hack the cold.

Through the open kitchen doorway, he's got his back to me, shirtless so I get full a view of his glorious tattoos, as he slaves over the grill. I take a seat at the kitchen nook.

He looks over his shoulder. "About fucking time. You sleep like the dead."

Lorcan comes over with a mug of steaming coffee. He leans close to place it on the table. Although we sometimes sleep in the same bed, he doesn't kiss me. He hasn't touched me since we moved in here except to hold on to me when he has nightmares. I don't know whether to be relieved, or frustrated. But if I'm honest, I'm fucking confused.

This is why I don't fucking date. I don't *what the rules are*

"I should be coming with you," I tell him as he moves away, leaving behind the coffee. I'm done with waiting, hiding. *I need release.*

What kind of release?

His green eyes narrow at me as he dishes up what he calls breakfast onto a plate. "We agreed to wait. Do you want one rasher or two?"

"I'm not eating that," I say, eyeing the grease and animal fat as I sip my scalding hot coffee.

He shrugs. "More for me."

"Is that bacon?" Dino, blue eyes twinkling, appears in the doorway looking devilishly handsome in his new school uniform in Royal Deacon red and black. He sees me and grins, sauntering in to steal a piece of bacon from Lorcan's plate.

Lorcan scowls as he tucks into his mountain of food. "For crying out loud, make your own fucking food."

"Where's Jude?" I ask Dino as he leans in to kiss me on the cheek like he does every morning, smelling of citrus shower gel and cinnamon. Unlike the dark-haired boy glaring at us both, Dino has no such qualms with touching me.

"In the shower. You know how he likes to use up all the hot fucking water." Dino strides over to the kitchen sink and turns on the hot faucet.

A yell from upstairs echoes through the house.

"Every fucking time," Dino smirks.

Lorcan rolls his eyes and shoves his plate into the sink. Then he disappears from the kitchen to finish getting dressed.

Dino pours himself a coffee waiting until we're alone. He catches my eye. "Casanova sleep in your bed last night?"

"He crawled in at 3 a.m." I shake my head, rubbing my temple. "He's fucking with my REM."

Dino releases a breath. "Since he's not allowed to bring girls back, he's using you as his support system."

I raise a brow. "He sleeps around because he's afraid of the dark?"

"At least he's not trying to screw you."

I don't say anything because I don't agree with that comment. *Screwing has benefits.*

Jude appears minutes later, golden blond hair still wet. His pretty hazel eyes give me a shitty glance as he enters, making it clear he'd rather I was dead in a ditch somewhere.

I sip my coffee and give him a cool look in return. *Asshole.* He's still upset that I tricked him, even though I also lied to everyone else. I don't even know why he's here, he's only on board with this because of Lorcan. I'm also pretty sure he convinces himself the same about me.

"Are we ready to leave?" Jude asks, slipping his black and red blazer on, the colors complement his coloring. He catches me staring and he smirks. In response, I recross my legs knowing his eyes can't help but be drawn to them.

Every morning it's the same. The boys ogle me and head out, and I sit at home and fucking count floor tiles.

Well, not today.

It's their first day, after the unfortunate events at Sacred Heart, that they're attending the school they've elected to transfer to for the remainder of the year.

Verity Hawthorne also elected to attend Royal Deacon.

I should be going with them.

"We're waiting for Lorcan. Then we'll head out," Dino says glancing between the two of us. Our hostility toward each other amuses the fuck out of him. "You guys should just fuck already."

I get to my feet. "You guys fuck. I'm going to get dressed." I leave the room to the sound of Dino chuckling to himself.

I dress quickly and insert some contacts, green this time, and then brush my newly dyed hair into the right kind of style. The boys are in the hallway when I enter it. Despite not wanting me to come with them today, they waited.

Lorcan's tie is off center, but apart from that slight irregularity, he looks hot as fuck. My body reacts by making my mouth water and my core tighten. *Damn that boy.* If he shows up at 3 a.m. again tonight, I'm going to restrain him and fuck his brains out.

"She's not coming." Jude, a storm brewing behind his eyes, opens his mouth first.

"I so fucking am."

Lorcan flicks his gaze over me, assessing my look. Finally, he nods. "Fine, but I say who we target. Do not go running amok the first fucking day." He turns away to walk out of the house without a backward glance.

"I hate that you had to dye your hair," Dino says as he matches my stride, coming up next to me as we walk toward the car parked in the external garage.

Jude is hanging back while Lorcan is already behind the wheel. I have a couple of seconds to say what I want with no one listening in.

"What the fuck is wrong with everyone?" I say, glancing at Dino. "Lorcan's pissed. Jude wants to kill me. This is not what I signed up for."

Dino cocks a brow. "You really don't know?"

"Enlighten me."

"You haven't chosen one of us yet," he smirks. "We've waited a month and it's fucking killing us."

"You're joking, right?"

Dino's mouth turns up at the corners. "I wish I was. We've agreed not to touch you until you decide."

"Jude too?"

"Why do you think he's so bitchy right now. Poor fucker's wound up so tight, he's going to crack. He's not used to abstaining. He needs to get laid." He leans in to whisper in my ear. "Secretly, I've been hoping you'll pick me, and we can finish what we started in the woods, feisty girl." He winks, and walks on ahead to claim the front seat.

. . .

Royal Deacon is ornate and decorative in its collegiate architecture, standing wider and grander than Sacred Heart in every way.

We pull up in Jude's Aston Martin. The steps leading to the entrance are littered with students. Everyone stops and stares. Lorcan and Dino exit first. Jude next, handing his keys over to the valet. And lastly, me.

My boys open my door and I step out of the car. No one takes my hand or offers their arm. They know better.

I start up the stone steps, boys not far behind me.

Standing at the top is a grim-faced Saskia. "Get the fuck away from me," she spouts at some guy harassing her. She slaps his hand away, looking a menace in black and red.

"You heard my sister," Lorcan snarls. "Piss off."

In my pocket is the notebook with the target circled in red between its pages. Strapped to my thigh is the blade I'm going to gut him with. Standing with me are the boys who get to clean up my bloody mess.

And etched into my bloody heart is who I've decided will be mine.

Lucky for them.

———

ALSO BY MALLORY FOX

WICKED HEARTS AT WAR

A Dark MF Stepbrother Bully Romance

War Of Hearts

Wicked Hearts

Hearts Break

A VIOLENT AGENDA

A Dark RH Serial Killer Romance

A History of Violence

A Legacy of Sorrow

A Promise of Torment

A Destiny of Carnage

MARKED

A Dark RH Capture Romance

Marked for Death

DIE FOR YOU

A Dark RH Mystery Romance

You Consume Me

STANDALONES

Sinful: *A Dark MF Teacher Student Bully Romance*

Gods May Cry: *A Monster Fae Romance* (writing as Lea Jade)

ABOUT THE AUTHOR

Mallory Fox is addicted to tatted up bad boys, chocolate covered pretzels, and looking deep into heart-melting, big brown eyes... the canine kind.

She loves to write deliciously dark romance with wicked, twisty plots about tainted-love, sweet revenge, and all kinds of emotional-rollercoaster redemption.

Mallory currently lives in London with her bean-shaped dog and the rest of her non-furry family.

Find more Mallory at facebook or sign away your soul at malloryfoxauthor.com/newsletter.

#wickedwordswithheart